ROLLING THE R'S

Carl —

ROLLING THE R's

Aloha

R. Zamora Linmark

R. Linmark
3.19.98
Berkeley

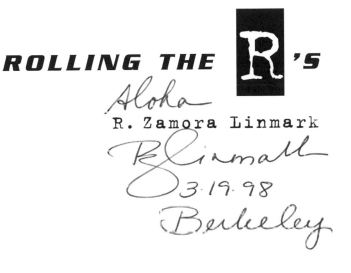

KAYA PRODUCTION

KAYA PRODUCTION
8 Harrison Street, Suite 3
New York, NY 10013

Second Printing, 1996
10 9 8 7 6 5 4 3 2

Book Design: Yuko Uchikawa / MAKERS' STUDIO
Jacket Illustration: McDavid Henderson

Manufactured in the United States of America

Distributed to the trade by D.A.P./DISTRIBUTED ART PUBLISHERS
636 Broadway, 12th Floor / New York, NY 10012
(800) 338-BOOK

Library of Congress Catalogue Card Number 94-75595
ISBN 1-885030-02-9

For your support, encouragement, and critical eyes and ears, I thank you: Faye Kicknosway, Jessica Hagedorn, Walter K. Lew, Lawrence Chua, Juliana Koo, Robert Kuwada, Sunyoung Lee, Lisa Asagi, Justin Chin, Lois-Ann Yamanaka, Trisha Lagaso, April Abe, Dommy Solomon, and Hyon Chu Yi.

I would also like to thank the editors of the following journals and anthologies in which some of the stories and poems in this novel first appeared, oftentimes in earlier versions: *Charlie Chan Is Dead: An Anthology of Contemporary Asian American Fiction, Willow Springs, MUÆ: A Journal of Transcultural Production, Ladlad: An Anthology of Philippine Gay Writing,* and *The Philippine Free Press.*

for Frank V. Linmark and Fernando Zamora
and in memory of
Steven R. Barris (1947–1995)

...and thus it will go on, so long as children are gay and innocent and heartless.

J.M. Barrie, *Peter Pan*

Skin, Or Edgar's Advice To Closet Cases

So what? Like me teach you how for French kiss, make hickeys, and M&M, too. Dumb ass, not candies. Mutual mastication, hand-to-hand resuscitation. Learned 'em from *Afterschool Special* with Mr. Campos and late-nite TV. Not Johnny Carson or Wolfman Jack. More like Pinocchio, grown-up version. The one that says: When he lies, it's not his nose that grows. Yeah, my parents know I watch skin-flix. Take NoDoz, Folgers, Coca-Cola. What they goin' do? Send me Kaneohe Hospital with the loonies and lobotomies? More like Hotel Street, 3 a.m.

Last night, I had sex with Scott Baio, Leif Garrett, Matt Dillon, too. We was workin' it, free for all, rough take. Scott was in my mouth and Leif was in Scott's, and Matt was in his briefs, lyin' on his side, same pose he had in the hayloft scene in *Little Darlings*. He was smirkin' at us, throwin' us that what-the-fuck-you-lookin'-at look. Of course was one dream, stupid head. You think Scott and Leif gonna go down on their knees, suck tongues and ding-dings, too? And Matt, you think that butch babe gonna go Hanes-naked and watch us play lollipops and roses? Shit, he rather oof Kristy McNichol. Of course was one dream. But you know what was so weird? While Matt was piggybackin' me to the bathroom—we was stark naked, of course—we saw you in the corridor givin'

1

Parker Stevenson the Hardy Boys treatment. You actin' like you knew the ropes by trade, spreadin' your legs for spill out the one-and-only clue. You was so grown-up, you knew who you was, and was lovin' it too.

BLAME IT ON CHACHI

Edgar Ramirez is a faggot. Mrs. Takemoto knows it. She's always telling him to stop putting his hair behind his ears.

"And cut your hair, Edgar," she says. "It's getting long again."

Edgar Ramirez is a faggot. Christopher and Rowell, the fifth-grade bulls, know it. They're always tackling him in flag football.

"A flag for a fag," they say. "Fag flag."

Edgar Ramirez is a faggot. Nelson and Prudencio, the other fifth-grade bulls, know it. They're always shooting him with their slingshots or tripping him each time he walks by swaying his hips hula-style.

"What, cannot walk without heels?" they say.

Edgar Ramirez is a faggot. Caroline, Judy-Ann, and Maggie, the Hot-to-Trot girls, know it. They're always fighting over him because he looks like a Filipino John Travolta.

"Edgar, you wanna come over my house?" they ask at the same time. "We can play Chinese Jacks," Caroline says. "We can read my *16* or *Teen Beat* magazines," Judy-Ann says. "We can listen to my Peaches & Herb tape," Maggie says.

Edgar Ramirez is a faggot. His mother and father know it. They're always grounding him because he spends all his money on life-size John Travolta or Shaun Cassidy or Scott Baio posters. And pins them up on the walls, ceilings, doors, in his father's workout room, and next to the altar.

"Anak, go to confession," his devout mother says. His father doesn't say anything. He just grabs the gardening shears and chops at Edgar's hair until he's bald, or burns the posters and shoves the cinders down Edgar's throat.

Edgar Ramirez is a faggot. His friends Katrina, Vicente, Loata, Mai-

Lan, and Florante know it. Even Edgar himself knows it.

"Since when, Edgar?" Katrina asks.

"Ever since I saw my father naked," he says.

"So what are you going to do about it?" Vicente asks.

"Nothing," Edgar says. "Nothing."

Blame my parents. They started 'em. First I was Totoy.

"Go give daddy a hug, Totoy."

"Come, Totoy, come kiss daddy bye-bye."

"No, Totoy, that's bad. Yes, Totoy, baaaad. Only mama can do that to dada."

"Yes, maaama."

Then one evening, while we was watchin' *Happy Days,* the episode where Chachi kiss Joanie for the first time, my father wen' call me all my names and other names too, just like I one schizophrenic or somethin':

"Totoy-anak, don't sit too close to the TV or you'll go blind," my father said. "Edgie, I said not to sit too close to the damn TV before you go baaalaaind! Punyeta, do you want me to turn the TV off? Don't but-it's-Scott-Baio-dad me, Edgar. Move it before I smash your head," he said. "Move, or else. What, Edgardo? What, Totoy, what did you say? Who taught you that f-word, Edgar? Answer me, Edgardo 'Totoy' Caban-ban Ramirez. I said, answer me. Okay, you wanna play deaf, go play deaf in your room. And from now on, I don't want to hear anymore Scott Baio or Chachi from your filthy mouth. Do you want your classmates to start calling you a fag? A mahu?"

At school the names they call me always come with one nudge or one punt, usually from the Filipino O.J. Simpson and Kareem Abdul-Jabbar wanna-be's, like Christopher Lactaoen, Rowell Cortez, and Prudencio

Pierre Yadao.

"Eh, you guys, check out that Fag, Edgar."

"What, Mahu, what you starin' at?"

"No act, Panty, before I give you one good slap."

"What, Bakla, you like beef right now?"

"C'mon, Homo."

"Right here, Sissy."

"Edga's ooone faaag. He like suck one diiick."

I swallow the names like the vitamins I gotta take before I go school. The pink-colored pills my mother stuffs in bananas cuz they supposed to make me grow big and strong. But when Christopher them start gettin' outta hand with the names, and their nudges start for turn to bruises, I roll up my sleeves and turn into the Queen of Mouth and Sizes.

"You guys think you so so tough, so so hot cuz you the youngest ones in the Kalihi Valley JV football team? Win one game first before you guys start actin' all macho. No shame or what? Why not pick on your own size, Tiny Tims? That's right. You guys are small, and I mean small, like the vienna sausage your mothers fry every mornin'. I know mine's bigger than yours. C'mon, pull down your pants. What, scared? Scared cuz mine's bigger than the three of you put together? Bust 'em out then. C'mon, no need be shame. Bust out those teeny-weenies. What, gotta have one microscope for look at your botos? C'mon then, prove how big and strong you really are. What you guys waitin' for? Bust 'em out so we can put you guys in *Real People* with Sarah Purcell. No, even better, *That's Incredible!* and have Fran Tarkenton introduce you guys as the junior jocks with microscopic cocks."

PROOF #1: QUEEN OF ICE PACK & CURAD

In the courtyard, I the Sham Battle Queen to re-enact what Florante calls the Fall of Bataan. Feelin' elegant in my Dove shorts I wear like one

French-cut bikini, like Cheryl Tiegs in *Sports Illustrated*, I skip to the battlefront with one red ball as my tiara, and pose as Queen of Atomic Words.

"Eh, everybody, everybody, I got one story to tell. Once upon a time there was two boys and a bathroom. One day, an angel named Edgar spotted them jerkin' each other off. They was goin' at it like cats and dogs. For real, I no kid you guys, brah. If you no like believe, go ask Prudencio and Christopher what they was doin' yesterday after school between three and three-thirty at the C-building bathroom.

"Eh, fuck you, too, Christopher-wanna-be-Kareem. I got better stories for invent than watchin' you and Prudencio jack each other off. With my own eyes and ears, brah, I saw and heard everythin'. Shit, even Helen Keller can hear all that moanin' and groanin' you guys was makin'. Prudencio, no be givin' me that stink-but-innocent look, like you don't know what the hell I stay talkin' about cuz I saw you, dumbass. When I heard noises comin' from one of the stalls, I wen' climb up the urinal for check out the view. And the view I got was better than the Pali Lookout. With my own brown eyes, I saw you, Prudencio Pierre-my-Cardin, goin' down on Christopher and makin' all that drownin' sounds. How did it taste, Pierre? So mahulani, I tell you."

I drop my ball to try for catch the rubber grenades attackin' from all sides, but they stay comin' at me at a hundred miles per hour to sting my face like one swarm of bees. I duck, of course, but as usual, I end up runnin' straight for the clinic where Mrs. Sugihara christen me Queen of Ice Pack and Curad.

But the next day, I march back to the court in my skimpy PE clothes for be the I Shall Return Queen.

PROOF #2: QUEEN OF CONTRABAND BOOKS & WHISPERS

"Hey, Katrina-Trina, here's Judy Blume's *Wifey*. You better not mark it or show it to everybody else like you did my *Forever.* What you mean 'no'? You such a liar, Trina. Had your red pen marks all over the ne-ces-sarry parts. Next time, just take notes, or better yet, circle the page number. No have to damage my books. Expensive, you know, especially now cuz of in-fel-lay-tion. You no watch Walter Cronkite or what? What you mean only the price of oil goin' up cuz of the OPEC guys? Now it's more worse cuz of the American hostesses in Iran. See now, I lost my thought of train. Oh yeah, damagin' my books. Yesterday, I found this book in Honolulu Bookstore. The Adult Section, of course. Where else? The Children's? Anyways, it's triple worse than *Forever* and *Wifey.* It's super-perverted. There's fuckin' in almost every chapter. And the way she describe the guy's dick is so unreal I can almost see it. No, you no can read 'em now. Finish *Wifey* first, but you better not mark that book, or else you never goin' see *Looking For Mr. Goodbar.*"

After school, before I turn into the Queen of Wide World of Sports, I stay in the utility room playin' Rejuvenation Queen for Mr. Campos, the custodian of the century. He say I make him young again. I tell him he make me feel so so mature. I lie, of course, cuz I no can tell him I rather do the splits for his young son who drive one mean-assed white bug with a bad stereo that vibrate throughout the valley. He's such a hunk. Like a cross between Dirk Benedict and Sly Stallone.

PROOF #3: QUEEN OF AFTERSCHOOL GYMNASTICS & DONNA SUMMER

"Eh, you guys ever seen one Filipino Nadia Co-ma-nee-chee? C'mon then, let's go to Loata's house cuz he get the best clothesline for swing on. Trina, you got your tape or what? No, not the Peaches & Herb tape. I tired do the uneven bars to 'Shake Your Groove Thing.' That's only good for floor exercises. Bring the one, you know, the one, the theme from *The Young & The Restless.* It's more better, more a-pro-pri-yate."

On afternoons when I no can be the Queen of Clothesline Gymnastics, I the Queen of Disco Divas.

"Katrina, you think I can pass for Donna Summer? What you mean, 'Gloria Gaynor'? Fuck you, Trina. I no look like Gloria Gaynor. What you mean cuz I get one afro. Eh, girl, my hair ain't no afro. It just look like one. What you mean Donna get one afro too? Fuck, Trina, you talkin' bubbles. Donna no more afro. The word is full, Trina, not afro. Eh, at least I no look like one white monkey like Alicia Bridges, like somebody I know. That's right, Trina. You look like Alicia Bridges. Maybe you guys twins, ah? No get all habuts on me, Trina, you the one who started it. Besides, who's the one who always tell me I sound like Donna Summer, especially when I sing 'Bad Girls'? No tell me Florante cuz he no even listen to disco. What you mean he does? For your information, Trina, Florante listen to kundimans, not disco. Big difference, you know. And no tell me was Vicente or Loata, either. Eh, if you like stay my friend forever, no start twistin' my words around and make like I the one who's at fault, okay? Okay. C'mon then, play one song already so we no make ass when we enter *America's I Love The Nightlife* dance contest. The judges strict, you know. They professionals, that's why."

PROOF #4: QUEEN OF DANCE FEVER

"Vicente, try feel my face. Smooth, yeah? Shut up, Trina, I talkin' to Vicente, not you. And don't ever ever tell me that I scrub my face, Trina. The word is d-fo-lee-yate. At least I no use SOS like somebody who get one a-bray-sive face. Anyways, Vicente, you ever tried playin' footsy under the table? You know, foot-c. That's what the haoles do in the movies before they oof. Like this. Shit, Vicente, you supposed to enjoy it. You supposed to re-c-pro-cate. Never mind, already, you not as smart as I thought you was. Eh, Katrina. Trina? Trina, fucka, no fall asleep on me. We next, you know. You ready for blow 'em away or what? You better make sure you got the steps downpacked cuz I no like make A, like the last time. Screw this one up, Trina, and I goin' find somebody else for be my dance partner. Just remember, first comes the sunshine, then the moonlight, then the good times, and then, the boogie. You got it? Better be, bumblebee."

PROOF #5: QUEEN OF CATECHISM, ROLLERWORLD & VIDEO GAMES

"Who says I hate my mother for makin' me go catechism class? You guys just jealous cuz I goin' straight to heaven. How I know? Cuz Father Pacheco told me so. He said, 'Edgar, my son, you keep doin' whatever you're doin' and you won't need to take the test when you get to Him.' Why, just cuz I go catechism, you think I goin' turn like one of them Jehovah Witnessesses? Screw you guys, you never ever goin' find me knockin' on your door just for tell you for twenty cents that you goin' burn in hell cuz you masturbate. Forget it. I worth more than that. You really like know why til this day, I still go catechism? Cuz Mr. Lee, my catechism teacher is one fox, that's why. And after every class, he take us Rollerworld, Farrell's, and to the movies. And we no gotta pay anythin' cuz he overly rich, plus he get one nice car. That's why I go to catechism. Last week, in fact, we went for see *The Amityville Horror*, and after that, he took us to the new Mitsukoshi building down in Waiks where we spent all his money playin' Galaxian and Space Invaders. That's where I saw the baddest hapa-babe I ever seen in my entire life. Now, all God gotta do is answer my prayers."

At night, after playin' Queen of Hail Mary, I stare at Scott Baio thumbtacked on my door with the valley breeze flappin' his pants. I slip between the cream-colored sheets and under the blue comforter my mother wen' order from Fingerhut, the one with the alphabets, then I flick off the lamp. In the dark, I feel the big letters and I start for write my name and all the names people call me. Faggot. Mahu. Queen. Bakla. Queer. Cocksucker. Dicklover. Even though most of the names are who I am and what I do, they say 'em with so much hate, like I ugly or some-thin'. But I not ugly. I might be mean, but that's cuz I need for be strong when they tryin' for put me down and make like I the one ugly cuz I not like them.

I close my eyes hard

and Scott Baio stay kissin' me I kiss him back

I feel Mr. Campos' chapped lips, his pomaded hair and greasy face

my father peepin' through the keyhole, murder in his eyes I tell Mr. Campos for get off me Quick

get off me get off me

I wake up like I no can breathe. Like my father was chokin' me. I stay sweatin' like I the one who got the DT's and not him. I change my clothes and jump back into bed

I in one white bug cruisin' around Waikiki with Mr. Campos' son We stay listenin' to Donna Summer's *Bad Girls* 8-track tape He steer the wheel with one hand and smoke Kool Milds with the other I move my Nadia legs slightly apart, like one perfect V Then I fling my head back and my arms out and make pretend I Nadia after a perfect landing He throw the cigarette in the air I catch his hand as it slides between my legs I play with his fingers

We in the old Pali Road It is pitch black and dead quiet I put his thumb in my mouth and suck it like one Sucrets lozenge The car move at caterpillar speed until it veer to the side of the road

I see the tree where Morgan hung himself I see Morgan's ex-girl-friend laughing I scared

No be I hea I take care you

He eject the tape for play my all-time favorite Peaches & Herb song,

"Reunited" He massage the nape of my neck
    I fall back he climb on top of me
    he press his lips we dry-kiss for long time
    my mouth slow
    ly
    his tongue in one circle after circle I fall
    in' with each circle
    full raw new like Chachi kissin' me
    for first time.

LIPS

Exotica is a woman trapped in a foreigner's body. Like Jodie Foster trapped in her mother's body in *Freaky Friday,* except Exotica is a man from the waist down.

"I keep it neatly packed in a nylon stocking and pull it out in case of emergencies," Exotica tells Edgar and me. "It is such a nuisance, honey. It feels like a huge mole."

She draws out a blusher from her makeup bag and accentuates her cheekbones until they look as if they're ready to pop. Then, "I'm just waiting for D-Day to come when the doctors cut it off so I can finally straighten out my act. In the meantime, I'm contented with my adopted twins," she says, petting her breasts.

"If ever I had one pair," says Edgar, "I like 'em be full as yours, Exotica, but they gotta be petal-shaped and bloomin'." He breaks out into an Arnold Horseshack laugh.

"Do the men you go out with ever know what you really are?" I ask.

"I try to be discreet about it," Exotica says, spilling the contents of her makeup bag onto the vanity. "It's such a bother—I have to spend hours and hours just wrapping it up and tucking it tight between my legs."

She picks up a black kohl eyeliner and paints her eyes Egyptianesque like Elizabeth Taylor's in *Cleopatra.*

"Have you always wanted to be a woman?" I ask, watching Edgar stretch out his shirt to examine his chest.

"Since the day I saw the light," Exotica says. "I even have my own theory on why I am the way I am."

"What is it?" I ask.

"Well, I always knew deep inside me that I was made to follow in Sister Eve's footsteps, but my mother hated apples. In fact, she was allergic to them, especially mountain apples. That's why I came out a boy instead of a princess," Exotica says, giving them her revised version of Creation.

"Although to be honest with you, honey, I don't know why I had to be one of the chosen few." She pauses to grab the mascara. "I don't know what forces impel me to be this way, and I'm not just talking about putting on a dress and makeup, or deceiving men either."

She twists the cap open and begins the task of combing and lengthening her lashes until they spread out like spider's legs.

"It's got to do with feelings, honey, *feelings*," she continues. "At first I went through my guilt-trip episodes, but those were a centuries-old program, if you know what I mean."

"How did you finally accept yourself?" I ask, staring at Exotica's reflection in the mirror.

"I woke up one morning and realized I was pretending to be something I could never be—a man. Honey, let me tell you, it was the worst acting stint I'd ever done in my whole entire life. It made me feel so uncomfortable and cheap, I get goose bumps just thinking about it."

She catches me staring at her and throws a smile through the gilded, oval mirror. "Anyway, to make a long drama short, I finally had to choose between being miserable for the rest of my life, or beautiful. God knows where I'd be right now if I'd continued pretending."

"Probably the same sanitorium as me," answers Edgar.

"You're probably right." Exotica picks up a lipstick and stretches her mouth into an oblong shape. Edgar and I watch the reflection delicately paint red arcs.

"Exotica," Edgar says, interrupting her concentration, "you think you can make my eyes look like Liza Minnelli's in *Cabaret?*"

"Why?" she asks, snatching a tissue and pressing it between her painted lips.

"So I can come famous," answers Edgar.

"It's the lips that make a person famous, honey," she says. She turns to us and holds up the tissue as if she were displaying the Shroud of Turin.

"Not the nose, cheeks, ears, tits, legs, nor eyes," she says. "They say eyes speak a thousand languages, but the lips, honey, the lips hold a million secrets—and it's the secrets that attract attention."

"Is that how you get men to go home with you?" I ask.

"No, honey. I wait for them to stumble out of the bars. Once they start log-rolling on the pavement, that's when I take off my pumps, lug one over my shoulder, and whistle for a cab."

"You think my lips hide a million secrets?" asks Edgar.

Exotica examines Edgar's lips the way a fortune-teller reads cards. "Your lips aren't full enough to carry the heavy weight of enigma. But you have a beautiful pout—a princess pout."

"What's that?" Edgar asks.

"Very ambitious, manipulative, and powerful," Exotica replies, her eyes fixed on Edgar's lips as if there are more traits to foretell. "In short, honey, you come from a kingdom full of excitement and danger."

"Cuz I get one princess p—"

"A king never wants his daughter to possess too much power," she interrupts him. "But he also doesn't want to make her unhappy because once he does, all she has to do is unwind her long, braided hair and use it as a rope to climb down the tower and escape. In the end, he's left with no choice but to grant his daughter's wishes."

Taking pride in his newly discovered asset, Edgar tightens his pout until the lines around his mouth show.

"That's a no-no, honey," warns Exotica. "Pout like that and everyone, including the king, will mistake you for a wicked stepmother, or a plebian's daughter with a monkey overbite."

"What about my lips?" I ask, drawing them closer together until they're shaped into a small O. "Are they full enough to carry mysteries?"

Exotica studies my lips.

"He get famous lips, yeah?" Edgar asks.

"The definite curves mean eternity," Exotica says, as if hypnotized. "The redness for birth—"

"Like in 'children'?" interrupts Edgar, puzzled.

"No, not children, but creativity," she replies.

"What else?" I ask.

"The fullness for..." She raises her eyebrows.

"For danger and excitement?" Edgar suggests, prodding her for an answer.

I look at Exotica's eyes, spellbound and watery. I know she's discovered the secret I'm trying to hide. I want to rip the lips off my mouth so she can say it's all a mistake and has to start again. But I feel my lips caving in, my teeth digging into flesh.

"The fullness for what, Exotica?" badgers Edgar.

"For a kiss that means beauty and sadness," she says. She snaps out from under the spell.

"What does that mean?" he asks.

Exotica turns to me. I want to run far away from her and Edgar, but my legs feel like rubber.

"What does that mean?" Edgar asks again.

"It's nothing important," Exotica says. She turns her back, looks at me through the mirror, and winks. "You have a beautiful smile," she says, "so quit biting your lips."

"I will," I say. "I will."

RATED-L

The movie is titled *Making Love* so it's rated-R. It stars ex-Angel Kate Jackson as Claire, a TV executive producer; ex-Rookie Michael Ontkean as Zack, a doctor; and *Clash of the Titans'* Perseus, Harry Hamlin, as Bart, the novelist.

Vicente lies. Tells his mother he's going over to Florante's to work on a school project. Extra credit if handed in early. He asks for money in case they decide to order pizza from Magoo's. Six blocks and ten minutes later, he's riding in the back seat of Chantelle's black Rabbit, next to Exotica blushing her cheekbones cotton-candy pink.

Florante lies. Tells Lolo Tasio he's going over to Edgar's because Edgar has commissioned him to start writing his biography. He asks for money in case they decide to order pizza from Magoo's. Ten minutes later, he's sitting between Vicente and Exotica, who's thickening her lashes with Cover Girl's 24-hour mascara.

Edgar doesn't lie. Tells his parents he's going to see *Making Love* because it received three-and-a-half stars. Because it's about a closeted married man who breaks his silence. His father throws a fit; his mother sneaks a five-dollar bill into his pocket. Ten minutes later, he's sitting on the front seat, occasionally turning around to watch Exotica paint her lips watermelon-red.

The show has already started when they enter the dark, crowded room. Exotica whispers to meet in front of the lobby when the movie is over. Before they find their separate seats, Zack and Claire have already moved into a newly bought home with a fireplace in the master bedroom. Vicente finds a vacant seat next to a man leaning close to the woman beside him.

Zack lies. Tells Claire there is nothing the matter with him. His job is stressful. It's made him tired and moody; that's all. He turns from her, does not tell her how Bart and he faced each other, bare-chested.

Bart lies. Tells Zack he doesn't believe in love or relationships. His writing comes first. It takes all his time, consumes all his energy. He likes Zack, but not enough. It's too much to handle, too complicated—and his writing comes first.

Claire doesn't lie. Tells her boss she needs time off. To save her eight years of marriage. A baby will do it. She confronts Zack, tells him he's shut her off from his life. She wants back in. For emphasis, she breaks the china but not his silence. It's driving her mad.

For a week, Claire leaves; out of town on business—a job promotion. For a week, Zack and Bart wrap their arms around each other. Making love in front of the fireplace.

The theater is dead quiet except for Zack's and Bart's breathing made crisp by the kindling. The man next to Vicente shifts in his seat. Vicente feels the hairs of the man's arm brush his skin. He imagines himself and the man in front of a fireplace with Zack and Bart. The four of them wrapped in each other's arms, watching the ritual of flames.

Zack doesn't lie. He breaks his silence, tells Claire he's been unfaithful. There have been midnight kisses; his name is Bart. But Bart is gone. Claire tells Zack there's still hope— perhaps a psychiatrist. She doesn't need sex. Zack says it wouldn't be fair to either of them.

The man rubs his arm softly against Vicente's. Vicente feels the hairs dance like reeds on a stormy night.

Claire doesn't lie. Tells Zack she's happy for him. Very happy. Because she's happy with Larry and their one-year-old son Rupert. She kisses Zack on the cheek. He tells her he's happy, very happy for her. Tells her he's happy with his new life and lover in New York City. Claire and Zack kiss and hug. Goodbye, Claire. Bye, Zack.

As the credits begin to roll, the first bars of the title track, sung by Roberta Flack, swim across the silent room.

Here, close to our feelings
We touch again
We love again

The man glances at the woman beside him, her eyes fixed on Zack's car coasting down the winding road. He slowly moves his arm away from Vicente's.

And now neither one of us
Is breaking

Vicente turns his head, drops his chin against his shoulder, and furtively watches the man watch the roundness of the woman's lips, how they tighten to form a smile.

Our Lady Of Kalihi

Virgin Mary lives at the top of Monte Street right below King Kamehameha School, but you don't have to be from Kalihi Valley to know that. You can be riding the skyslide in front of Gibson's department store, lining up to visit the USS Arizona at Pearl Harbor, going on a buta hunt at Camp Erdman, or climbing the thirteen deadly steps near Morgan's corner, but the millisecond you turn towards Kalihi Valley, or even think to, you see her: A woman walking out of a mountain carrying a baby in her left hand and a crystal ball in her right, her melancholy eyes always open, always gazing down.

She isn't like the other Virgins. She bears no fancy names like Regina Cleri or Medjugorje, or Maria del Monte, but simply, Our Lady of the Mount.

She doesn't talk to children like Queen of Fatima, who is also called Mama Mary, because her mouth is veiled with asbestos. She can't dance when you blast the car stereo and shine your headlights on her, like Mary in Diamond Head Cemetery, because her feet are bound by a fat green snake with a pitchfork tongue. She isn't Asian-looking like La Naval, whose almond-shaped face, high cheekbones, slanty eyes, and flawless gown earned her a free trip around the world. And she won't heal the sick like Our Lady of Lourdes or perform miraculous feats like Our Lady of Mediatrix of All Grace, who showered the earth with roses, because a year after she was proclaimed Our Lady of the Mount, a hurricane stormed into the island and turned it into a garbage dump.

The buffeting winds jolted everyone and everything, including Our Lady of the Mount, whose tin-foil tiara and head were flung out into the Pacific Ocean. For months she stood decapitated at the top of the hill, waiting for Father Pacheco to collect enough donations to buy her a new head. When she was finally given the chance to think and see again, the parish of Our Lady of the Mount Church was a penny away from filing bankruptcy, for her disaster-proof head cost more than an arm and a leg. It was so expensive it came with a free crown and a makeover fit for a Halston runway show: Sophisticated with the jaguar eyes of Bianca Jagger, pout of Sophia Loren, cheekbones of Lauren Hutton, arched brows of Brooke Shields, and the attitude of a Studio 54 Disco Mama.

As you grapple your way up Monte Street with a bouquet of roses in your hand, you wonder if this mascaraed diva ramping out of the mountain is the same one that spoke like a dream the first time you collapsed before her. In front of the green snake that grins at you from around her feet, you offer her the roses wilting in your hand and look up at her newly acquired face. She does not look at you sweetly or serenely as before, but points her catty eyes toward the ships anchored at Pearl Harbor, prowling to see which sailor will crown her Notre Dama de Noche.

KALIHI IN FARRAH

Everybody in Kalihi wants to be Farrah. The name itself sounds sultry and expensive. Who doesn't want to be the reigning queen of pin-up posters thumbtacked on every wall of the house? A swimsuit goddess with long and graceful legs, pearly white teeth, glossy lips, roller-derby hips, and a million-dollar smile on a king-size waterbed next to none other than the Six Million Dollar Man himself. Who doesn't want that full-volumed, sunshine-gold mane: Side-combed, feathered at the top, then curled along the sides? Who in Kalihi doesn't want to be Farrah?

◆

Ernesto Cabatbangan, a freshman at Sanford B. Dole Intermediate, doesn't want to be Farrah; he wants to be inside her. He bought all her posters on discount from DJ's Record Store because his calabash cousin manages the Pearlridge branch.

He says he can't get it up unless she's there watching over him, smiling. At times, it gets so bad that he sprays the room, bull's-eyeing Farrah's mouth.

◆

The two-hour season premiere of the hit series *Charlie's Angels*, starring ex-Rookie Kate Jackson (Sabrina Duncan), commercial model Jaclyn Smith (Kelly Garrett), and newcomer Farrah Fawcett-Majors (Jill Munroe) attracted 5,483,097.99 households, according to the Nielsen Ratings. A week later, Edgar Ramirez formed the Triple-FC, the Farrah Fawcett Fan Club, with him acting as the President, Katherine Katrina-Trina Cruz (1st Vice President), Caroline Macadangdang (2nd Vice President), Jeremy Batongbacal (Secretary), Judy-Ann Katsura (Treasurer), and Loata Faalele (Sergeant at Arms).

The Triple-FC's primary goals were to keep the TV show on the air and the blond bombshell's career alive. This meant watching every episode including reruns, wearing T-shirts with Farrah Fawcett iron-on stickers, buying the Jill Munroe doll, playing the *Charlie's Angels* board game, trading *Charlie's Angels* cards, and praying the novenas every Wednesday with Father Pacheco at Our Lady of the Mount Church.

Once a week, the club met at Edgar's house to: 1) write letters to Farrah Fawcett c/o ABC Network; 2) show off their collections of Farrah memorabilia, including cut-outs from glamour magazines and Farrah's latest swimsuit poster; 3) role-play scenes from *Charlie's Angels*; and 4) discuss socio-politically charged issues raised by the show, such as prostitution, lesbian undertones, and Orientalism.

When Farrah left the top-rated show, they continued their Farrah piety, anxiously waiting to see her movie *Sunburn*. Unfortunately, it got scorched by bad reviews and a month later, Triple-FC wrinkled up.

♦

Orlando Domingo's favorite letter is F, not F for Filipino, but F for Farrah, and he won't answer to his friends and classmates who call him Orlando, his teachers who address him as Mr. Domingo, or his mother who nicknamed him Orling.

"Just call me Farrah," he says, "as in Far-Out Farrah, or Faraway Farrah."

It all started with *Charlie's Angels* and his addiction to Farrah's blond mane. One night he borrowed his mother's box of curlers and did his hair before going to bed. When he woke up, he propped himself in front of the vanity and blow-dried, at extra-high speed, the rows of hair caged in pink. Then he removed the curlers and began the arduous task of styling his locks into the million-dollar mane coveted by Farrah wanna-be's and Flip queens.

"Farrah, Farrah, what's the secret to your hair?" the Filipino Farrah wanna-be queens ask him. And all he says is, "Once a Farrah Flip, always a Farrah Flip." Or, "A Flip is a Flip is a Flip." Or, "Secret."

"He's flipped out," Orlando's classmates at Farrington High tell each other the moment he enters the classroom sporting Farrah's hairdo. "The next thing you know, he goin' be packin' on makeup and dressin' up like her, too."

Sure enough, the day after the *Charlie's Angels* episode titled "Consenting Adults"—the one where Detective Jill Munroe goes undercover as a call girl and delivers her immortal line of "I-never-give-anything-I-can-sell"—Orlando struts into class wearing a fire-engine red polyester long-sleeved shirt tied around his 24" waist, yellow bell-bottoms, and Famolare platforms. His face is painted, courtesy of Helena Rubinstein's The Paris Boutique Kit, which includes lipstick and nail lacquer, and Aziza's Shadow Boutique. Twelve shimmering eye colors for every occasion.

"What next?" the teachers ask during their lunch break. "Principal Shim must do something about this. Ahora mismo!" The following week, after Orlando views the episode called "The Death of a Roller-Derby Queen," he wheels onto campus on black leather Cobra skates, wearing see-through Dove shorts, red Danskins, and red-and-white knee and elbow pads. And, as always, fully made-up with Farrah's hairdo that withstands the Kalihi breeze with the aid of an entire can of unscented Aqua Net hair spray.

"We gotta do something before our boys catch this madness and start huddling in skirts and pom-poms," the football coaches Mr. Akana and Mr. Ching tell Principal Shim. "You gotta do something. Pronto.

Suspend him, expel him, we don't care, but you gotta keep him away from our boys if you want the team to bring home the OIA title."

Leaning back in his vinyl chair, Principal Shim considers the possibility of expelling or suspending Orlando on the grounds that he is endangering the mental health of other students, especially the athletes. But he can't. Not after he examines Orlando's file:

> Born in Cebu in 1962; Immigrated to Hawai'i at the age of ten; Lives with mother in Lower Kalihi; Father: Deceased; Speaks and writes English, Spanish, Cebuano, and Tagalog; Top of the Dean's List; Current GPA: 4.0; This year's Valedictorian; SAT scores totaling 1500 out of 1600; Voted Most Industrious and Most Likely To Succeed four years in a row; Competed and won accolades in Speech and Math Leagues, High School Select Band, Science Fairs, and Mock Trials; Current President of Keywanettes, National Honor Society, and the Student Body Government; Plans to attend Brown University in the fall and eventually take up Law.

Principal Shim closes the file and throws it on his desk.

"I can't expel him. Maybe suspension." He squirms at the thought of Orlando turning the tables and charging him, Mr. Akana, Mr. Ching, and the Department of Education with discrimination against a Filipino faggot whose only desire is to be Farrah from Farrington, as in Farrah, the Kalihi Angel.

REMIXING
AMERICA

Toot toot, hey, beep beep. Toot toot, hey, beep beep. Hey, bad girls, hey, bad boys, and all you nasty bad queens. Toot toot, a-ha. A-put on your dancin' shoes and head on down to America. It's my joint, your joint, his and his joint, her and her joint, it's everybody's joint. Come check it out. America's got everythin' your heart desires: Dancin', pinball, fooz-ball, dancin', skee-ball, Pac-Man, dancin', and more dancin'. Buy a slice of pizza, get a medium-size Coke free. Seven days a week, three hundred sixty-five days a year, America's dancin' on your beck-and-call. This is the home of the brave and the wild and the free. Be free, sweat it out, get loose, get funky. Shake shake shake, shake shake shake, shake your booty, shake your booty on America's newly renovated dance floor, equipped with the latest hi-fi system. This is the right place and the right time for that right catch. So if you want his body and you think he's sexy, roller skate on down to America, sugar, and let him know. Yowsah yowsah yowsah, ahhhhhhhhh freak out! le freak, c'est chic. Stand, kneel, spread, squat, push push in the bush, you know you want to get down. Push push in the bush, fine by me if that's what you're into. But if you're into love, baby, everlasting, romantic, dramatic love, baby, America is flooded with, ahhhh, love to love you, baby. Ahhhh, love to love you, baby. Come lay close to me, baby, for there's no place I'd rather you be than, ahhhh, love to love you, baby, than here in America, ahhhh, love to want your lovin', baby, love to want you want my lovin', too. I miss you, baby, miss you so much. Ever since we last saw each other here in America, all I've been doin' is thinkin' about you, about you dancin' beside me to guide me, to hold me, scold me, and even spank me, baby, cuz when I'm bad, I am so so bad. Oh baby, I just wanna feel your body close to mine. So, come, fly into my arms, let me know the wonder of all of you. Don't be afraid, don't be petrified, and don't throw away that key or change that stupid lock cuz tonight, baby, we're gonna make up and do more than just do the hustle and talk about love. No sweet-potato talkin', baby. Strictly one hundred percent pure action. My body, your body, everybody loves somebody, and even if you have that special some-one, bring him along, too, so while you try me, try me, try me, try me one more time, I can try him, try him, try him for the very first time. I can just see it now, baby, the three or four hundred of us groovin' on the dance floor, eye-to-eye, skin-to-skin, our flesh touchin' sky, our minds floatin', our tongues dancin' in circles. We, are, fa, ma, lee. I got all, my sisters, brothers with me. Our souls funkyin' to the beat of the lights, lip-synchin' to save the last dance for Donna and to remind ourselves that if Gloria can survive, so can we, cuz we were born, born, born, born to make that move, right now, baby, born to make us feel mighty real. Oh, baby, I'm burnin' up, baby, my dancin' soul's on fire. Burn, baby, burn, disco inferno. Ahhhhhhhhh, baby, you started this fire down in my soul, can't you see it's burnin' out of control. Why not groove on down to America tonight, baby, cuz I promise you, baby, I promise, I'll satisfy the need in you forever and ever. That's right, baby, cuz that's the way, a-ha a-ha, I like it, a-ha a-ha. I want you, baby, need you, baby, need you to get you and your friends down here tonight. So all you restless kids age ten and above, put on your dancin' shoes and boogie woogie oogie on down to America. On the corner of Nimitz and Sand Island Access Road. Doors open at seven. See you here tonight, baby. I'll be waitin'.

Bino And Rowena Make A Litany To Our Lady Of The Mount

Hail Mary, Mother of Christ

Mother of Christ

Mother of the Cross

From the Cross Jesus gave you to us

The kindest, the most loving

Mother of all

We thank you Lord, our Holy Trinity

Father of heaven and earth

For giving us your own Mother

Mother of Perpetual Help

Mother of all sinners

Mother of all mothers

Who should be seen and not heard

Mother of all children,

Who should be seen and not heard

Have mercy on us

Give us strength for our daily bread

Most Immaculate Mother

Mother of weights and barbells

Holy Virgin of virgins

For it's you to whom we plead

Mother of Divine Grace

For it's you who we need
To ask God to have mercy on us
Have mercy on us
Mother most pure
Queen of Camay
Mother most chaste
Queen of Lysol
Mother most flawless
Queen of Revlon
Mother undefiled
Queen of Generals
We pray for our country
The land of our birth
Have mercy on us
Mother of Chancellors
Queen of all queens
Have mercy on us
We pray for all nations
For peace to all nations
Have mercy on us
Mother of all ears
Mother of good counsel
Mother most admirable
Mother most honorable
Virgin of thy Father
Maker of heaven and earth
Virgin most kind
Virgin most powerful
Virgin most loving
Virgin most venerable

Virgin most asked-for
Virgin most merciful
Virgin most blessed
Mother of orphans
Mother of Annie
Pray for her
Mother of Madeline
Pray for her
Mother of Wonder Woman
Pray for her
Holy Sister of Mrs. Garrett
Pray for her
Holy Sister of Betty and Veronica
Pray for them
Holy Sister of Marcia, Jan, and Cindy
Pray for them
Mother of Ambassador of Goodwill
Mother of Gary Coleman
Pray for him
Mother of Buck Rogers
Pray for him
Mother of Erik Estrada
Pray for him
Holy Sister of Fred and Barney
Pray for them
Holy Sister of the Jackson 5
Pray for them
Mirror of Justice
Queen of the Superfriends
Pray for them

Mother of all things
In heaven and earth
Queen of Longs Drugs
Pray for us
Queen of Castle Park
Pray for us
Queen of VISA, Mastercard & American Express
Pray for us
Queen of 5-star hotels
Pray for us
Mother of Ronald McDonald
Pray for us
Queen of the Vatican
Mother of Archie Bunker
Most High of all Highnesses
Queen of Eiffel Tower
Tower of David
Tower of Pisa
Queen of all Angels
Kelly Garrett
Sabrina Duncan
Jill Munroe
Queen of Slinky
We pray to you
Our spiritual vessel
Vessel of Salvation
Vessel of Devotion
Vessel of Martial Law
We pray to you
Lift up your hands

We lift them up
Most Glory of all that is glory
Open your mouths
We give you praise
Most Noble of all that is noble
Lead us to the gates of heaven
Queen of Pac-Man
Queen of Space Invaders
Queen of Centipede
Carer of the sick
Shelterer from famine
Guardian of Luke Skywalker
Holy Mary, Mother of God
Pray for us
Queen of Martyrs
Queen of all wounds
Mother of my mother's bruises
Pray for her
Mother of my father's belt buckle
Pray for him
Mother of my mother's barbed-wire lips
Pray for her
Mother of my father's high kick
Pray for him
Mother of my mother's tetanus shots
Pray for her
Mother of my father's two-by-four
Pray for him
Holy Queen of all queens
Queen of Mercurochrome

Queen of bandages
Queen of a thousand excuses
Queen of sick calls
Queen of thirty-eight stitches
Queen of ICU
We come to you
Holy Mary, Mother of God
Mother of all mothers
Now and at the hour of our death
Amen.

Encore

In the Philippines, Vicente De Los Reyes was Christopher De Leon and his sister Jing was Nora Aunor, the country's best actor and actress. This year Jing retired from their faux show business. She said she was getting too old for that kind of stuff. Too busy, too actively involved with the Key Club, the Fil-Am Club. Plus she's a JV cheerleader. Plus this. Plus that. So Vicente replaced her with an ensemble which includes Edgar, Katrina, Loata, Florante, and Mai-Lan.

The stage is a low, thick stone wall that separates Mr. Batongbacal's house from Mrs. Freitas's. Two or three times a week, they climb up the wall to perform sold-out concerts like *Bee Gees: Live In Kalihi*, or scenes from box-office hits like *Grease* and television shows like *Charlie's Angels* and *The Facts of Life*.

The main audience includes: Vicente's brother Bino; Bino's friend Rowena; Mr. Batongbacal, Vicente's landlord, who watches from behind the kitchen curtains; Mrs. Freitas, who watches Mr. Batongbacal from behind her living room curtains; and Roberto, Mrs. Freitas's son, who watches from the garage while he waxes his yellow Plymouth between guzzles of beer.

This past week was a replay of the Grand Prix finals of *Dance Fever*. Starring Edgar Ramirez as Deney Terrio, Loata Faalele as the video disc jockey Freeman King, and Katherine Katrina-Trina Cruz and Vicente De Los Reyes as Dianne and Toni, otherwise known as The Motions. The special musical guest was Grace Jones (Edgar) who sang "Do Or Die." The three special judges were...

First, one of the hottest young TV actors working today. We all know him as the handsome older brother of Arnold Drummond from the hit show *Diff'rent Strokes*. Please give a warm welcome to Todd Bridges (Florante);

Next, the actor who could write a book on cross-dressing in the military. He makes us laugh every Friday night as he plays Corporal Maxwell Klinger in the Emmy Award-winning series *M*A*S*H*. Give a round of applause to our second judge for the evening—Jamie Farr (Bino);

Our third and final judge is the main reason why teenage boys want to spend their Friday nights sitting at home with their mothers. Everyone across America knows her as the feisty Lucy Ewing from the hit soap *Dallas*. Please welcome the sexy, the vivacious, the Princess of Prime-time Soaps, Ms. Charlene Tilton (Rowena).

The first finalists were a couple (Edgar and Katrina) from Flint, Michigan, who danced to Dan Hartman's "Instant Replay." The next finalists were a husband-wife team (Edgar and Vicente) from the heart of the Big Apple. They touch-danced and dipped each other to "Bridge Over Troubled Water" by Linda Clifford. The third finalists were twin brothers Shawn and Shane (Edgar and Edgar) from Fire Island, New York, who wowed and won the crowd with their (his) dramatic disco interpretation of Donna Summer's "MacArthur Park."

While they wait for Edgar to make his appearance from around the corner where he is squatting behind Mrs. Freitas's plants, Vicente catches Roberto's eyes darting at him as he waxes his car. Vicente looks away, pretends he doesn't see Roberto's eyebrows go up to form thick lines across his forehead; instead, he turns to Bino and Rowena who sit cross-legged on the lawn, reading *Madeline* books.

"Edgar," Katrina shouts towards Mrs. Freitas's house, "come out of the bushes already cuz we turnin' into fungus over here."

No answer, though she knows he'll pop up from the potted plants as he always does. He once told Katrina that he has to stall for time and must always be the last one to show up because he is *the lead* star and *the lead* star never shows up early or on time.

Edgar makes his dramatic entrance as Venus surrounded by bougainvilleas, with his arm around a boom box and a duffel bag on his shoulder. He wears an ear-to-ear smile and his favorite Angel Flights bell-bottoms, Famolare shoes, and a T-shirt. Sprawled across his chest is an iron-on sticker of Andy Gibb.

He throws one hand in the air, the signal for Katrina and the others to scream and pretend they just spotted their favorite idol incognito. He hurries towards them and rests the boom box and his duffel bag on the stone wall.

"You guys never goin' believe this," Edgar says.

"What?" Vicente asks.

"Yesterday, I went to the dentist for a check-up," Edgar says.

"So?" Katrina says.

"So the whole time I was there, I was forced to listen to elevator music," Edgar says, referring to KUMU, the all easy-listening station, twenty-four hours a day.

"So?" Katrina repeats.

"So no get wise before I punch your face," Edgar says. "Anyways, you guys never goin' believe the kind songs I was hearin'."

"Like?" Loata asks.

"Like the instrumental version of 'More Than A Woman,' 'I Love The Nightlife,' 'Got To Be Real,' 'Boogie Wonderland.'"

"Nah," Loata interrupts.

"For real," Edgar says. "I no could believe myself. Anyways, when I got home I called up KUMU and requested all these songs."

He unzips his duffel bag and pulls out a tape. "I spent the whole night listenin' and recordin' all the songs I wen' ask the DJ for play," he says. "Except for 'Love to Love You Baby.' That one he never had, but he had all the others."

"Like?" Vicente asks.

"Like 'Makin' It,'" he says.

Katrina screams. It's hers and her babe Erwin's theme song.

"And 'On The Radio,'" Edgar continues.

Mai-Lan gasps.

Edgar turns to Florante. "And," he pauses, "I also got 'Do That To Me One More Time,' Florante's favorite Captain and Tennille song."

"What else?" Vicente asks.

"And 'Enough Is Enough.'"

"No way," Vicente says.

"First song on this tape, brah," Edgar brags. "And this goin' be the first thing we goin' sing and dance to. And cuz I so so nice, I goin' sing the Barbra Streisand part and let you sing the Donna Summer part even though I sound just like her."

"But I don't know all the lyrics," Vicente says.

"No worry," Edgar says, producing two *Song Hits* magazines from his bag.

"What about the words to 'Makin' It'?" Katrina asks.

"I get 'em, too," he says. He turns the bag upside down. A beaver dam of *Song Hits* piles up on the stone wall.

He hands Vicente a magazine. Vicente pages to the table of contents. "Enough is enough is enough is enough," he starts singing.

"Wait," Edgar says, "I not ready. And you not ready either."

"Why?" Vicente asks.

"Cuz you not on the stage, dummy," he says, handing the tape over to Katrina.

They haul themselves to the top of the wall. Edgar gestures to those below him, reminding them to applaud once the song begins.

Silence.

Silence.

"Katrina, start the freakin' song, dumbass," Edgar shouts.

Katrina obeys.

Silence then static.

"Dolby," Edgar hisses. "Put it on Dolby."

The music starts: Piano, violins, flutes, harps.

"Shit, Edgar," Vicente says. "When you said instrumental, you didn't tell us it was going to be the forest version."

Edgar walks over to the cassette recorder and turns it off.

"What you expected, stupidhead?" Edgar shouts. "The Studio 54 mix? We talkin' KUMU here, not KIKI or KKUA. You so ingrateful sometimes."

"Yeah," Katrina seconds. "Just shut up and sing. At least Edgar's idea beats lip-synching. Besides, now we can really positively know for sure if you get one choirboy voice like you always brag about. Plus you should be thankful he makin' you sing the Donna Summer part."

"Okay, I get the message," Vicente says.

Edgar rewinds the tape and once again reminds the audience to please applaud.

The song begins with a piano prelude (Florante, Loata, and Mai-Lan applaud), violins (Katrina screams), flutes (Rowena tears up). Opening lines are Edgar's. He hums to Rowena and Bino, then tells them that it's raining, pouring, and his love life is boring him to tears.

He turns to Vicente, who's sweating cats and dogs as he tries to resurrect a voice dormant for almost a year. "No sunshine, no moonlight, no stardust, no sign of romance, no nothing," Vicente quivers.

"Use your imagination, Donna," Edgar lip-tells Vicente, then pauses when he catches Roberto's eyes fixed on them. Edgar turns to Roberto and flies him a kiss. Roberto flashes a grin as his hands continue to wax. Edgar flies him another kiss. Roberto throws the rag aside, leans against the trunk, crosses his arms, and listens to Edgar recount to him that he once dreamt he had found the perfect lover but he turned out to be like every other man.

Vicente leans over to ask him why is the beat not picking up. Edgar half-closes his eyes, begins gyrating, then tells Vicente again to use his imagination.

Vicente joins him, echoes that it's raining, pouring once again, and that they're not going to hang around waiting to shed another tear. He closes his eyes and imagines singing to the original disco version he dances to at America discotheque and not the one that will accompany him to the cemetery.

He imagines that Edgar, Katrina, Loata, Florante, Mai-Lan, Bino, and Rowena are not there. No Roberto's eyes. No Mr. Batongbacal or Mrs. Freitas behind their curtains. He shakes his hips, lets loose his choirboy voice. "Enough is enough is enough is enough is I've had it."

Surprised by Vicente's rich voice, Edgar tells him, "Sing it, Donna."

Altoing loud and clear, Vicente imagines strong hands kneading his neck, his shoulders. He stretches his neck to the right, to the left, then back, then forward, the way one does when being massaged by someone like Richard Hatch or Jan-Michael Vincent. He opens his lips and offers his song to the sky.

Katrina sees Vicente's father's car driving into Mr. Batongbacal's driveway. "Edgar," Katrina says, pulling his pants.

Eyes closed, Edgar, who's imagining that he's just been betrayed by Scott Baio, shouts to Katrina: "I want him out I want him out the door now goodbye Mister."

"Edgar," Katrina says, shaking his legs.

Edgar opens his eyes to Mr. De Los Reyes's face heating up like a volcano about to erupt. He vaults down from the stone wall, shoves the *Song Hits* into his duffel bag, turns off the music, and walks away with his boom box and bag. Katrina and the rest follow him, except for Bino. Roberto, who's gone back to waxing his car, starts whistling.

With eyes still closed and imagination wide open, Vicente sings to his father. "I can't go on no longer because enough is enough is enough is I gotta listen close to my heart. Wooooo-wooo-wo."

Mr. De Los Reyes climbs up on the wall and grips his son's neck, wrenching it until Vicente snaps free of his imagination. Then he pushes him off the wall. Bino rushes to Vicente, who's fallen on his hands and knees. But Mr. De Los Reyes has jumped down from the wall and is pulling Vicente up by the hair, shoving him away from the stone wall and the curtain of eyes trailing after them.

The Eyes Of Edgar Ramirez

My first tiltillatin' experience was in third grade. Real far-out kind sensation, like my body was one roller-coaster ride. My eyes was open and I could see everythin', but everythin' wasn't definite. Pretty sure was third-grade time cuz *Charlie's Angels, Bionic Woman,* and *Wonder Woman* all premiered. They made my dreams more adventurous and super-vivid. Like the time I dreamed I was Lindsay Wagner, and I was bionic, battlin' and winnin' against asshole wanna-be machos like Christopher and Rowell. I wish I was bionic everyday so I no gotta have to give that extra push just for be myself. Nights was safe then, until I saw Linda Blair as Regan in *The Exorcist.* Ho, that movie wen' freak me out so bad that I wen' turn super-religious. I started for attend mass every Sunday, and I wen' even sign up for be Father Pacheco's altar boy and enroll in Mr. Lee's catechism class every Wednesday after school. I no like end up one atheist like Linda, that's why. I mean, I no mind seducin' one hot-to-trot priest in Latin but not while my head stay doin' three-sixty and my eyes lit green. After *The Exorcist,* I told myself the worst of the worst is over and no scary movies can ever give me nightmares again. I was wrong cuz right after *The Exorcist,* Exotica wen' ask me if I like go see Stephen King's *Carrie* at the Royal Theater on Kuhio Avenue. "Shoot," I told her. Then she wen' warn me over and over that it was one horror movie but

I told her, "No Worry, X, I can handle." Scary or not, I had to go cuz her friend Chantelle told me that they was wearin' awesome prom clothes and one of the actors was this hot babe named John Travolta who kinda look like me. From start to finish, I stay strapped on my seat, prayin' like hell. I no could stop screamin', especially at the end part where Carrie's hand pops out of the ground in front Amy Irving's face. I was so shook up, Exotica had to snap me out of it. Up til now, I still get my Sissy Spacek nightmares. They so scary and bizarre, like the time John Travolta wen' dump one bucket of pig's blood on Sissy at the prom, and my father come out of nowhere for tell John, "Eh, John, the dinuguan, John. What a waste! We could've eaten pig's blood for dinner." Thank god Donna Summer rescued me by releasing her latest album *A Love Trilogy* and her disco version of "Could It Be Magic." Spirits move me, ev'rytime I near you. Good, yeah, my a cappella? Whirlin' like cyclone in my mind. My father loves for whistle that song only cuz he one Barry Manilow fanatic, especially when he stay soberin' up. He no really care that much for Donna; he say to me all the time, "Just watch, Edgar, that chick goin' turn conservative on you."

I decided for stay home that day cuz Ms. Chun was takin' the class Kodak Hula Show again. One visit was sufficient, but five times in one year was too much. I wanted for slap her face each time we went there. I finally figured out that the reason she took us there was cuz she one pake to the max and Kodak Hula Show no charge admission. So freakin' tirin' for have to sit, listen, and look at a bunch of tourists go monkey over 'Pearly Shells' and 'Tiny Bubbles.' More worse, she wen' make like never had other places for go. Lucky thing the field trip was on one Thursday, cuz Wednesday nights get *Charlie's Angels*. Used to come on real late before, right before *Baretta*. Still had Farrah then, before she ditched Jaclyn and Kate for pursue her movie career. Felt sorry for her cuz she get actin' potential too, but she had for make *Somebody Killed Her Husband*

and *Sunburn*. I told my mom light one candle for Farrah.

Anyways, I woke up to *Match Game* that mornin', my bladder ready for bust. I wen' run to the bathroom, half-asleep, and right there, at close range, was my father, butt-naked, blow-dryin' his hair. His boto not like Long Dong Silver, but was no Vicks Inhaler either. Was fat, middle-finger size, pubes to the max. He wen' act normal, said, "Go ahead, Edgar, pee all you like. I almost pau." He never even tried coverin' up. So I sat on the toilet, took my time. I no could pee for shit. Had to concentrate real hard cuz his ass was right there in my face. I closed my eyes and tried for think of somethin' else, but no matter what, I no could resist stealin' one glance at his ass and his balls danglin'. My body felt like one sauna. Blood rushed to my head. I thought I was goin' faint. I could hear my heart thumpin', like the thing ready for jump out of my chest. I wen' look down and caught my hard-on. And just when I wen' cross my legs, he wen' turn his head to me for say, "You pau piss or what? I like use the toilet." "Yeah," I told him, "I almost pau." He wen' turn back to face the mirror, and started whistlin' Morris Albert's "Feelings." I know I had to leave. I wen' push my hands down underneath my belly button hard for try make the piss come out but never like. So I just wen' flush the toilet real fast so he no could see that I wasn't pissin' the whole time I was sittin' there. I wen' stand up, tryin' for look real calm even though my body was real sore and my dick was still hard, then I wen' rush out the bathroom. Felt funny, just like one comedy the whole thing. But felt scary and good feelin' at the same time.

You Lovely
Faggot You

You, in the dark, if only he could see you, take the time to touch you, work his want into your skin because the night is young, raw, volatile; if only he could run his hand on your face, show you how something beautiful can be something dangerous can be something passionate; if only he could take your hand high in the air, spread your fingers to the night, bring it closer to his face until all you feel is his face, ah, his face, how you'd sink your palm on his face, massage his brows, how you'd press it hard on his eye so he could see the river of lines rich with salt, how your fingers would trail from the bridge of his nose down to his mouth, half-opened, hungry, thirsty, how you'd trace his lips, map out where the want ends and the need begins, where the desire to taste salt moves him closer to you, his arms around you, his mouth heavy on your neck, his tongue sanctifying your sweat, how you'd open your mouth and swallow the night that only you and he have come to understand and accept and know as something once forbidden now sacred; if only he could hold you until daylight creeps in to break your arms chained with safety; if only he could tell you that what he says and what he does are the same as what you feel and think, then and only then would you let go of his embrace, because the night would return to comfort your skin and worship your flesh, then and only then would you feel reassured that the night that you and he have come to want and take and need is very much alive and young and raw and any fears of daylight begging for the door to open wider are suppressed by a kiss that lasts longer than a sigh and a passion that comforts your existence; if only...

Good luck. I hope you find Prince Charming soon because if you don't, you'll end up sleeping in some bell tower next to your sewing kit and heaps of magazines on crocheting, embroidery, and quilt patterns. What are you doing in the dark, anyhow? Waiting for the IF man to come galloping into your heart and take you away to his fortress? Big dreams. Let me tell you something: IF is a boil on the ass, a mean hangover, retinitis, and unless you've been screwed over you wouldn't know whether to go fish or cut bait; IF is for those who live in Lalaland fenced by giant billboards with broken Christmas tree lights and a mailbox loaded with rehearsed lines; IF is for melodrama queens who hold vigils til five in the morning, their eyes weeping and rolling to the sky, wishing for a star to fall so they can make a wish and wish it comes true. So cut the crap and turn the lights on before you turn into fungus. What makes you think that a star is going to fall on you, anyway? Go jerk yourself off to sleep and hope you don't wake up with a headache.

THE THREE QUEENS

Diana is a fat mole
a third almond eye
between Mirabella's silicones
knuckles of Everest
flesh of the Ganges

in heat
Diana is a silver hoop
a cockring
cuffed on Chantelle's tongue
sacred sighs of the Great Wall
milk of the Yangtze

in heat
Diana is a stud in drag
a blue pearl
rammed down Exotica's throat
thick fist of Taal
ancient crown of Pasig

in heat
three very flaming queens
pout their banana-do-me lips
scratch their panties
under a red light
Mirabella sells his soul

to Mr. Faust of Frankfurt
skates between Hitler's mustache
and a beaded sanskrit

under a red light
Chantelle rents his jaded tongue
to Monsieur Le
Fleur of Montparnasse
kneels between La Seine
and an immigrant's harelip

under a red light
Exotica leases his cinnamon lips
to Mr. Jones of Pasadena
douches between Walt Disney's
ears
and a sidewalk scapular

and crouched before
altars red with flowers
three mothers
in sacred heat
pray their rosaries
bead by bead
their tongues on fire

Tongue-Tied

Ms. Takara visits the class once a week. On Thursdays. Before fifth-period Social Studies, which is actually History and not the extension of lunch recess that Florante and Vicente thought it would be when they first heard the course title.

Always dressed in a muumuu with an arc of plumeria or hibiscus flowers pinned to her hair, Ms. Takara can pass as a model for Hilo Hatties or Liberty House, though Florante tells Vicente that the flowers in her hair are so huge she looks like Nagasaki, blooming.

When the fourth bell announces the death of lunch recess, Ms. Takara is at the door ready with her konnichiwa smile while Mrs. Takemoto threatens her students to *settle down, kids, I said settle down before...*

Katrina and Edgar see Ms. Takara and Mrs. Takemoto as the Japanese versions of Sabrina from *The Archies* and Broom Hilda. Mrs. Takemoto is the four-eyed Broom Hilda: Middle-aged, obake-looking, with a husband who prefers to sleep with Katrina's mother. Ms. Takara is the double-lidded Sabrina: Young, beautiful, and a professional back-stabber because she is too nice to be true.

Florante thinks that Ms. Takara is two-faced: A Japanese and an American wrestling in one mind. He says that her American upbringing has blinded her from reading between the lines of the history textbooks where silenced people choke from invisibility and humiliation.

For Mai-Lan, however, Ms. Takara is a guide, a once-a-week fairy godmother who takes her away from the Nelson Ariolas of the world for forty minutes to deposit her in a red room. There she can open her mouth without Nelson telling her that she speaks English like she's got a plugged nose. With only Ms. Takara, Vicente, and Florante listening, she feels more at ease, unashamed to express herself. Words come out like a free-flowing river. No pauses, no hesitations, no tongue too embarrassed to release the right Englishy words. And no need to think American to speak English because, to Mai-Lan, language is not words, but rhythms and sounds.

Once Mrs. Takemoto has quieted the class for the beginning of fifth period, Florante, Mai-Lan, and Vicente leave Mrs. Takemoto's classroom with Ms. Takara. They pass the library. Down two flights of steps. Across the small courtyard where Stephen Bean was crowned Christopher Columbus on Discoverer's Day.

They pass the D-building bathroom, the office, the janitor's room, the health room, then enter what Florante calls the asphixiating room. It reminds him of the colonial history of the Philippines—from Magellan's three-hundred-year-old crucifix to President McKinley's hallucinations to Tsuneyoshi's camps to MacArthur's shades. And he never fails to point out the irony of Ms. Takara wanting to remove him, Vicente, and Mai-Lan from class to teach them a thing or two about integration.

Except for the light that peeps through the wooden louvers, the room, which is used for arts and crafts by kindergartners and special ed students, is dark and musty. At the center is a tiny table with tiny chairs; chewing gum sticks like stalactites underneath the table. A black cable used to hang children's palms imprinted on white construction paper runs across the room. Along the walls painted with Crayolas and felt markers are bookshelves and cubbyholes storing children's books, Play-Doh, and art supplies. Three bean bags sag onto the red carpet blotched with Elmer's glue, fingerpaint, and Bubble Yum.

While Mrs. Takemoto is burying her students' heads in Plymouth Rock or George Washington's cherry tree or the big migration to the West, Ms. Takara checks up on how Florante, Vicente, and Mai-Lan are adjusting to their newly adopted home. She asks them how they spent their weekends, or what they want to be when they grow up.

TREATMENT 1

Think V. Valley, not balley. Va, va, valley. Deliver, not deliber. Not da liber. De, de. Liver. From, not prrrom. Evil, not ebil. Deliber, deliver. V's not b's. Fly, not ply. Not punny, but funny. Funny, not punny. Fun, not pun. Filipino, not Pilipino.

PROGRESS NOTES

TO THE PARENTS:

This report is intended to give you an approximation of the progress of your child during this school year 1979–80.

Your interest in, and understanding of the school progress of your son or daughter or twins will be an important factor in his/her/their success. The school cannot accomplish much without the cooperation of the home.

We hope that you will welcome an opportunity to confer with your child's/children's teacher regarding his/her/their school progress.

Principal Okimura

PUPIL: De Los Reyes, Vicente
GRADE: 5-201
TEACHER: Mrs.Takemoto/Ms. Takara

SCHOOL: Kalihi-Uka School
PRINCIPAL: Mr. Okimura
RDG LVL: Equivalent to H.E.P. 4th grade level
ATTENDANCE FOR 1ST QUARTER:
> Days Present: 45
> Days Absent: 0
> Times Tardy: 0

TEACHERS' COMMENTS:

Vicente is a happy child, a friendly pupil who is very neat in appearance. Ms. Takara and I especially like his flaming orange and green and purple jumpsuit. Before we forget, Ms. Takara and I would like to commend you for having such a very conscientious son, who, in our years of teaching, has the most beautiful and unique penmanship. However, Vicente also has a tendency to daydream in class, which gets him into trouble. If he isn't daydreaming, he's often busy reading *Tiger Beat* and *Dynamite* magazines, signing Slang Books, or talking while instructions are being given. Vicente needs to hand in his assignments on time; they are usually 2 or 3 days late. Will you encourage him to hand in his work on time? And will you also discourage him from associating with Edgar Ramirez and Katherine Cruz? Ms. Takara and I think that they are the primary cause of Vicente's inattentiveness. Vicente needs to gain confidence in himself.

Mrs.Takemoto/Ms. Takara

PUPIL: Phan, Mai-Lan
GRADE: 5-201
TEACHER: Mrs.Takemoto/Ms. Takara

SCHOOL: Kalihi-Uka School
PRINCIPAL: Mr. Okimura
RDG LVL: Equivalent to H.E.P. 2nd grade level
ATTENDANCE FOR 1ST QUARTER:

Days Present: 42

Days Absent: 3

Times Tardy: 2.5

TEACHERS' COMMENTS:

Mai-Lan is a happy child, a friendly pupil who is very neat in appearance. Ms. Takara and I would like to commend you for having such a very conscientious daughter, who, in our twenty years of teaching, has the most beautiful and unique penmanship. Mai-Lan tries hard to participate in class. However, she has difficulty following lessons because of her lack of English. As her understanding increases, her work should improve. Mai-Lan should also learn her +, −, x, and ÷ tables better. Ms. Takara and I understand that Mai-Lan is new to this country, but she needs to learn to control her emotions and to take her time when expressing herself. By doing so, she should be able to gain more confidence in herself and in her English. Ms. Takara and I also noticed that Mai-Lan constantly talks to Katherine Cruz while instructions are being given. Katherine Cruz only speaks pidgin, and Ms. Takara and I think that she is the reason for Mai-Lan's inattentiveness and worsening study habits. Will you discourage Mai-Lan from associating with Katherine Cruz? By doing so, her grasp of the English language should improve immensely. Mai-Lan also needs to try to come to class everyday and to be more punctual.

Mrs. Takemoto/Ms. Takara

PUPIL: Sanchez, Florante
GRADE: 5-201
TEACHER: Mrs.Takemoto/Ms. Takara
SCHOOL: Kalihi-Uka School
PRINCIPAL: Mr. Okimura
RDG LVL: Equivalent to H.E.P. 5th grade level
ATTENDANCE FOR 1ST QUARTER:

> Days Present: 45
>
> Days Absent: 0
>
> Times Tardy: 0

TEACHERS' COMMENTS:

Florante is a very introverted child who likes to read history textbooks and write verses during recess and lunch. He is very conscientious, meticulous, and, for lack of a better word, a true perfectionist. He also has the most beautiful and unique penmanship Ms. Takara and I have ever seen. However, Florante rarely participates in class and needs a good deal of encouragement. Will you help him gain confidence in himself? In his writing assignments, Florante uses English properly, expresses ideas creatively, uses correct spelling, and has an extensive vocabulary. Ms. Takara and I had the opportunity to read one of his verses and were surprised at how much it moved us. Though Florante reads with understanding, he needs to improve his pronunciation. Ms. Takara and I noticed that the other students Florante does associate with are Katherine Cruz and Edgar Ramirez. Will you discourage him from further associations with these two? Their use of pidgin endangers Florante's appreciation and skillful usage of the English language.

Mrs. Takemoto/Ms. Takara

TREATMENT 2

Think three not tree. Watch the r's. Think think, not tink. Th. Th. Th, th. Da ink. No: Th, th, th, th-ink. Think. Prrreee. F's, not p's. Frrreee. Do not roll the r's. Free. Three. Three. Free. Bery good. V. V. Very. I am Filipino, not Pilipino. Fil, pil. Fil. Fil. Fil, fil, filfilfilfil. Philippines, not Peelipines. My name is Plorante. Flo. Flo-rante. Florante. Prrrrom. Frrrrom.

The Battle Poem Of The Republic

by Florante Sanchez

I.

Last week, Mrs. Takemoto made us
write a poem in standard English
for the Annual State Poetry
Contest, Division III.

... if chosen, $100.00 ...

Our eyes went bonkers. Our faces
wore hundred-dollar smiles. Even
Katrina-Trina Cruz's packed-on
makeup and Judy-Ann Katsura's
scotch-taped eyelids were peeled
off by the crisp Ben Franklin.

... read your poem out loud ... top three ...

Christopher Lactaoen and the other
fifth-grade bulls strutted around
with an I-spit-on-your-poem attitude,
gave everyone the evil eye, especially
me. Eh, Florante off the Boat,
just cuz you one poet no mean you goin'

win first prize. No way, José.

II.

For one week, we were frustrated.
Line breaks, metaphors, similes,
haole-write English. But when sixth-
period PE came, we spilled out
our insecurities with sham battle,
German dodge-ball, flag football,
and every ball imaginable.

III.

When time came, everyone went up:

Rowell Cortez, the only Filipino who had enough courage to admit he ate black dogs, wrote 'bout his first time at a cockfight in Waipahu.

Mai-Lan Phan wrote 'bout coming to America and shopping at Kress.

Katherine Katrina-Trina Cruz wrote 'bout her third time with her babe, star quarterback Erwin Castillo.

Edgar Ramirez wrote 'bout being an altar boy and the fun he had with Father Pacheco who played with him and let him sleep over.

Vicente De Los Reyes, my best friend, wrote 'bout Edgar winning the semifinals round at *America's I Love The Nightlife* dance contest.

Jared Shimabukuro wrote 'bout winning the Chinese Jacks competition.

Christopher Lactaoen wrote 'bout his first time with Maggie Perez inside the big cannon in front of Fort DeRussy.

Caroline Macadangdang, Christopher's ex, wrote 'bout beefing Maggie after school in front of Kress.

Nelson Ariola, Maggie's ex, wrote 'bout giving Christopher a black eye after school in front of Kress.

Maggie "Honeygirl" Perez wrote 'bout her first hickey from Christopher.

Judy-Ann Katsura wrote 'bout being grateful that she's Japanese and not Okinawan like Jared.

Prudencio Pierre Yadao wrote 'bout surfing at the North Shore with the tsunami waves breaking the bones.

Rudy Rodrigues wrote 'bout his dog-tattooed shoulder.

Benjamin Fontanilla wrote 'bout the uninvited bees that wrecked his birthday picnic at Magic Island Beach Park and ate all the lumpias, pansit, and pig's blood.

Stephen Bean wrote 'bout the military importance in Hawai'i.

Loata Faalele wrote 'bout this road in the deep end of Kalihi Valley diverging and he could not figure out which one to take, so he took the path that was less familiar, and he ended up in Laie.

IV.

I wrote 'bout

Hungry bees eating space, black dogs losing it first time

America raiding scotch-taped Kalihi while Pedros drowned in Franco's German-spit second time

Dim in the Philippines, PI Joes missing in Fort DeRussy's dead-end pockets third time

Immigrants coming to Kalihi, dodging the American sham battle fourth time

Smiles that break evil bones after school, touch-dance brawling in front of Kress fifth time

Uninvited priests with dog-tattooed arms, grinding fighting cocks, and preaching last words sixth time

(And I wrote 'bout a pig cap pen bleeding a hundred-dollar poem.)

PORTRAITS

The best way to describe the Sanchez family is that they are all writers. Florante. His mother, Celia. And his grandfather, Lolo Tasio, who came from and brought forth a generation of writers.

They live a block away from Our Lady of the Mount Church on Machado Street, in a vine-covered house that is so old the paint has stopped peeling.

Dama de noches, which bloom only at night, trellis around the front and side windows, whose torn screens are petals about to fall. Behind the fence covered with stephanotis vines are sampaguita shrubs—the national flower of the Philippines—planted along the walkway leading to the front steps. Behind the house is a vegetable garden ripe with tomatoes, bitter melons, squash, and eggplants. A malunggay tree stands next to the garden, marking the soil in which it is planted as owned by a Filipino.

The front door of the three-bedroom house opens onto a library. Books thick as encyclopedias and old as the Bible run across three walls and are also stacked on the floor and along the corridor. Books written in Spanish, English, and Tagalog. In the center of the room is a typewriter on a Narra desk.

Thumbtacked on the wall facing the typewriter are three posters. A blindfolded Jesus wearing a barbed-wire tiara is crucified at the center; his lips are stapled shut. The head of the cross is inscribed with the date 1521. To his right is a map of the Philippine archipelago that is striped in red-white-and-blue and looks like the skeleton of a dog sitting upright; to his left is a cartoon of Mount Rushmore bearing the faces of George Washington, Thomas Jefferson, Ferdinand Marcos, and Charles Manson. Above their heads, in capital letters, is the phrase ALL IN THE FAMILY.

Florante unlatches the gate and leads Vicente to the back of the house. A man in a straw hat, white shirt, and brown trousers with the cuffs rolled up to the knees is watering the tomato patch with a sprinkler.

"Mano po, Lolo," Florante says, blessing his forehead with his grandfather's hand. "This is my friend Vicente."

"Good afternoon po," Vicente says.

"Good afternoon, hijo." Lolo Tasio sets down his sprinkler and steps forward to reveal a face that had seemed younger at a distance and under the wide brim of his hat. A face marked by lines and solitude. Vicente tries not to wince as his eyes are pulled by the deep scar running across Lolo Tasio's brow. A scar that could've only been formed by a sharp object—a knife, a chisel, the teeth of a dog.

Lolo Tasio extends his arm. Vicente grasps his hand and feels the calloused palm, its pronounced lifelines.

Drawn by this face ravaged by time, Vicente continues to gaze at Lolo Tasio. "Where are you from in our country, hijo?" Lolo Tasio asks, taking out a pair of glasses and wiping them on his dirt-stained kamisa de chino.

"Sa San Vicente po," answers Vicente.

Pleased by Vicente's insertion of the polite form of "po" in his Tagalog, Lolo Tasio smiles. "It's good that you haven't forgotten your Tagalog."

Hanging above the small dining table, in a gilt-edged frame, is a black-and-white portrait of Florante's family taken in front of the globe fountain in Luneta Park. The water spouting from the top of the huge ball looks like rivers of smoke running down the continents.

Vicente studies the picture. "This boy looks just like you. Is he your brother?" he asks.

Florante, who is at the kitchen counter preparing merienda, nearly spills the carton of chocolate milk he's pouring into a glass. "Yes, he is," he answers.

"Is he back in the Philippines?"

Florante hugs the two glasses of chocolate milk and the plate of condensed-milk sandwiches and sets them on the blue vinyl-covered table.

"Just you and your grandfather live here," Vicente persists.

"My mother is here," Florante pauses. "But the rest of my family—my younger brother, sister, father, and my Lola Neneng—they're no longer with us."

"Why, what happened?"

"They were shot."

"Shot?"

"They were walking home from the market one Sunday afternoon when a speeding jeep chased them off the edge of the road and soldiers started shooting at them. Our neighbor saw it all happen. She came running up to our house, screaming and crying and pulling my mother's hand, but by the time we got there, there was nothing to see but bodies covered with blood and bullet holes. After we buried them, we left the country."

"I don't understand," Vicente says.

"Some people didn't like what my grandparents and parents were writing about."

The screen door opens and Lolo Tasio appears, his face and back dripping with perspiration. "Hijo, did you check the mail?" he asks, removing his shirt.

"Hindi pa ho. I'll go check it right now," Florante says. "Vicente, why don't you wait for me in the living room? That's where the library is."

Vicente gets up to follow Lolo Tasio through the door that separates the kitchen from the body of the house. He hesitates a moment when he sees the geography of scars and welts imprinted on Lolo Tasio's back, reminding him of the men who, during Holy Week, hid their faces, tore their skin open, and dotted the road with their blood.

One Easter afternoon he and his maid Fely had snuck out of the house to follow the caterpillar trail of men who paraded around San Vicente, beating their bare backs with palm fronds or bamboo sticks. Though their heads were covered in T-shirts, everyone in the provincial town, especially the women, knew that they were the bodyguards of the Mayor.

"Yaya Fely, why are they hurting themselves?" Vicente asked his maid.

"They're asking God for forgiveness," answered Fely.

"Why, what did they do wrong?"

"They are not faithful to their wives."

A man broke out of the procession and handed Fely a razor blade. With his back to her, the Levi's-clad repentant knelt and ululated to the sky as Fely hovered over him to slice a wound.

Vicente's eyes continue to follow the scars running across Lolo Tasio's back, until they disappear as the old man enters a bedroom. Stopping by the endless shelves of books in the center of the living room, Vicente is suddenly overwhelmed. The posters pull his eyes towards the wall bleeding with bikini-clad martyrs, stone-headed presidents, and serial killers. He stares at Christ, whose wounds form rivers of blood, deep islands of pain that make him wonder about Florante's family that Sunday afternoon, how their bodies convulsed to the rat-ta-tat of gunfire before their tongues licked dirt. At the back of his head, he hears Lolo Tasio's typing and begins to imagine ghosts seeping from his fingers, telling him their stories plotted with perfect miseries and orchestrated deaths, and souls resurrecting higher, higher than Christ.

Requiem

Memory is a mosaic of tongues licking dirt, of lies embroidered to protect the King of Martial Law.

He was born. He is risen. He will kill again. And his kingdom will have no end.

Memory is a 1972 machine gun fired one Sunday morning. Four bodies on the edge of a road. An act of suspended drowning.

This is a cup of his blood, the new and everlasting covenant.

Memory is a woman who howls wolf past curfew. Late night dinner parties and spilled champagne.

She drinks it so that his sins may be forgiven.

Memory is a spinning bottle, a top with no base, a mad pack of white dogs eating brown tails, brown dogs eating spotted tails.

She breaks bread, gives it to his disciples, and says, Eat this in memory of us.

Memory is an archipelago of closed-view coffins, eaten calmly like sugared fingers of bread.

SOMETIMES THE D-BUILDING BATHROOM

Students are not allowed to use the D-building bathroom located right across from the basketball court. Principal Okimura declared it the D-zone, the danger zone, because that's where the DMG hangs out, Da Manong Gang, with black dog tattoos on their forearms and deep crucifix scars on their left temples. Although Rudy Rodrigues has a tattoo barking out of his right bicep, he has yet to earn the DC scar on his temple. "Da Cross, brah," he says. "Da Cross that means no can be chicken shit; means jump; means kill or be killed."

On gutsy days, Rowell and his fifth-grade bulls play DMDU, the Dare-Me-Dare-You game where they take turns running back and forth in front of the DMG's bathroom, peeping through the thick clouds of smoke to see if there really are big laminated posters of Farrah Fawcett and Jesus Christ tacked on the stalls. The game is cut short because the DMG leader Manong Rocky always comes out, sleepy-eyes all red and rolling, puffing Kool Milds and cracking his knuckles.

During class time, Mrs. Takemoto and her students hear spray cans rattling, noses sniffing like dogs. Sometimes they hear real dogs barking, yelping so loud it rings in their ears for days. And the smell, like burnt hair, is so foul that Edgar has to soak his body in Calgon bubble bath for hours. That's the DMG doing their Double-D thing. "First we beat the dog up with one mallet," Rudy says, "then we set the buggah on fire with one blowtorch, then we grind 'em." And on the night of the Double-D thing, Rudy has another chance at the crucifix scar.

After school, the DMG comes out and leans against the urine-splashed wall, smoking and cussing as they wait for the DFFM man. Da Filipino FM man who drives the red Continental with eleven rearview mirrors and hundreds of glittering stickers. The students also wait for the DFFM man. But they keep their distance, stick to their territory, lean against the torn fence or kill time playing H-O-R-S-E.

Sometimes the DFFM man doesn't come; sometimes he's late. But everyone knows when he's just blocks away because the valley shakes from the pounding of his car stereo. The students abandon their spelling hoops to rap to "Rapper's Delight" by Sugar Hill Gang or le freak to c'est chic. They turn their heads toward the tinted window, wait for it to roll down so they can see if the DFFM man really does have reptilian eyes and a chameleon's tongue like Rudy says. They get nowhere because the DFFM man always has his aviator shades on and a silk handkerchief over his mouth.

When fingers start snapping, he slides out of the car and Da Manong Gang leads him into the bathroom. Sometimes he brings a brown leather briefcase. Sometimes a woman dressed in a tight skirt, loose blouse, and high heels climbs out of the passenger-side door and follows the DFFM man into the bathroom. It's always the same briefcase, never the same woman. When he leaves, the briefcase goes with him, the woman stays behind with Da Manong Gang. "She stay with us til nighttime," Rudy says. "Sometimes she no go home til morning already. And sometimes," he says, "she no come out at all."

On most days when Rudy pops into class, he's high on the Triple-D, Da-Do-and-Die thing that dilates his pupils and wires his brain. He rolls up his sleeves and shows Edgar, Katrina, and Florante the needle-tracks, like bruised highways, running across his arms. At recess, he tells them about the 3-D's, the Dreams Dreamers Dream: Plenty of cash; A beachfront mansion for his mom; Jewelries for his sister Luisa.

On days when he comes to class not feeling sky-high, he sinks deep into his seat and re-tells the story of D&M. Daddy, who chickened out on Mommy, leaving her with Rudy, Luisa, and two jobs. "I just waitin' for run into that asshole," he says. He grabs the edges of his desk and shakes it hard until his entire body convulses. "I just waitin' real patiently cuz the moment I see him, that asshole goin' be dead. He goin' be one dead-meat," he says, and kicks the desk in front of him. "I goin' blowtorch him like the dog he is, man, blowtorch that asshole." Then he stands and kicks his desk over, and the desk behind it.

Mrs. Takemoto, Vicente, Mai-Lan, and the girls scurry out of the classroom to call Principal Okimura. Rowell and his fifth-grade bulls run to the other side of the room to hide under Mrs. Takemoto's table. And Edgar, Katrina, and Florante step back toward the windows that overlook the D-building bathroom, their gaze fixed on Rudy's slitted, snake-like eyes.

The Two
Filipinos

Mai-Lan Phan is Vietnamese.

Jared Shimabukuro is Okinawan.

Judy-Ann Katsura is Japanese.

Stephen Bean is Caucasian.

Loata Faalele is Samoan.

Caroline Macadangdang is one-fourth Filipino, one-fourth Spanish, one-fourth Chinese, one-eighth Hawaiian, one-sixteenth Cherokee Indian, and one-sixteenth Portuguese-Brazilian.

And the rest tell Mrs. Takemoto, who has gone row by row asking them their ethnicity, that they are Filipinos, except for Nelson Ariola, who says he is an American although he is as Filipino as any Filipino can be.

"No, Nelson," Mrs. Takemoto says. "Your nationality is American, but your ethnicity is Filipino."

"Yeah, Nelson," Katrina Cruz interrupts. "You was born a Filipino, and you goin' die a Filipino."

"Shut up, Katrina," Nelson says.

"You shut up, Nelson," she says. "What makes you think you not a Filipino?"

"Because I was born here," he says.

"So? Me, too," she argues.

"And because," he pauses, "because I'm not an immigrant." He glares at Florante and Vicente. "I don't speak English like I got a plugged nose," he says, shifting his eyes to Mai-Lan. "And because my grandfather never came here for cheap labor." He sneers at Benjamin Fontanilla, who, when he's not busy living in his own small world, tells his classmates stories about his paternal great-grandfather, Apo Lakay, who was a Sakada, one of the first Filipinos to arrive in Hawai'i to work at the sugar plantations on Kaua'i.

Benjamin raises his head, his eyes like cane knives on Nelson. "I pray my grandpa's spirit come drag you out of your mansion and bury you in one burning field," he mutters, bending his head down.

"That's enough, Benjamin," Mrs. Takemoto says.

"I'm sick and tired of being called a Filipino," Nelson says. "I'm not like them, Mrs. Takemoto."

"What makes you say that, Nelson?" she asks.

"Because I don't speak Tagalog or Ilocano...."

"Well, for your information, Mr. USA," Edgar stands up, hands fisted at his waist. "Your mother speak Tagalog and your father from the Ilocos. And just cuz you no speak the dialect no make you one overnight American sensation."

"Shut up, Edgar. You don't understand," Nelson says. "I can't be a Filipino. I don't want to be a Filipino because the only Filipino everyone knows is the Filipino that eats dogs or the Filipino that walks around with a broom in his hands."

"So what? Big deal if Filipinos eat dogs. Big deal if they custodians or gardeners. Besides, why you care so much about what other people think? That's their kuleana, not yours," says Edgar.

"Because I don't want to be called a dogeater or a gardener for the rest of my life," Nelson says.

"You're so full of yourself, Nelson. Just cuz your father one lawyer and your mom one nurse. Wake up and smell the hot pandesal. Windex your mirror cuz your reflection goin' tell you you the best candidate for Mr. Pinoy—brown skin, yellow teeth, and no nose."

Even timid Jared Shimabukuro, who rarely lets out a sound, laughs.

"Quiet down," Mrs. Takemoto says.

"Look at me," Edgar says, rolling up his sleeves to expose his tan-lines. "I a mestizo born in the U S of A, but my fair skin no stop me from the fact that I one Filipino."

"But it's not only the color of skin that matters," Nelson says. Edgar interrupts: "Exactly. Took you that long for figure out. So just accept the fact that you more flat-nose than me."

Edgar bows and sits down. Stephen Bean stands and crosses his arms. "Nelson, if you're such an American, then what am I?"

Nelson opens his mouth; no words escape.

"One haole, what else?" Katrina says.

"That's enough, Katrina," Mrs. Takemoto says.

"At least I have a father," Stephen says.

"You like me go over there and bust your face?" Katrina says.

"You started it when you called me a haole," Stephen says. "I'm not haole, I'm Caucasian."

"Same freakin' smell, dumbass," Katrina says. "You in Hawai'i and a Caucasian is a haole is a haole is a Caucasian. And if you no can handle the tropical heat, go back to Antarctica."

"Katrina." Mrs. Takemoto slams her hand against the desk. "If you don't stop, I'm going to report you to Principal Okimura."

"Oh, no be threatenin' me, Broom Hilda," Katrina says.

Edgar turns around to Vicente and chortles.

"Detention for one week, Katrina," Mrs. Takemoto says. "The rest of you better settle down, or you'll be scrubbing the floors and wiping the chalkboard with Ms. No Manners."

"You just wait," Katrina says under her breath, "you freakin' bitch. Wait til I tell my mother and Uncle Craig."

Edgar stands up and faces Stephen.

"Edgar, sit down," Mrs. Takemoto says.

"Why only tell me to sit down," Edgar says. "Why no tell the haole for sit down, too."

"Shut up, faggot," Stephen says.

"No tell me to freakin' shut up, haolitosis," Edgar says. "And Mrs. Takemoto, you open one case but you no can close 'em, so I goin' close 'em once and for all."

Edgar first points his finger to Nelson. "You, Mr. Haole Wanna-be," then points to Stephen; "and you, Mr. Haolewood. You guys think you so hot-shit, but you know what? The ground you standin' on is not the freakin' meltin' pot but one volcano. And one day, the thing goin' erupt and you guys goin' be the first ones for burn."

They Like You
Because You Eat Dog

They like you because you eat dog, goat, and pig's
blood.

They like you because you grind your women the way
you eat pulutan.

They like you because you drink, play mah-jongg, and
cockfight.

They like you because you go to church every Sunday.

They like you because you kneel hard, bend over quick,
and spread wide.

They like you because you worship blue passports.

They like you because you guard the exiled President's
body in Temple Valley.

They like you because your daughters date marines.

They like you because you machine-gun your own kind.

They like you because your sons smoke crack, cut class,
and sport tattoos.

They like you because you wear rainbow-colored
clothes, toupees, and can boogie.

They like you because you are third-world hip.

They like you because you have olive skin and yellow
teeth.

They like you because you say you're Spanish or
Chinese.

They like you because you have big tits and a tight ass.

They like you because you're the butt of everyone's
jokes.

They like you because you have a cock the size of a Vicks Inhaler.

They like you because your favorite fruit is banana.

They like you because you sell home-grown utong, kalamungay, and eggplants at the open market on Saturdays.

They like you because you're a potato queen.

They like you because you're one hell of a gardener.

They like you because you work three full-time jobs—scouring pots and pans, scraping greasy floors, and scrubbing toilet bowls.

They like you because you're a walking cholera, hepatitis, and TB.

They like you because you're too proud to collect welfare.

They like you because you are minimum wage.

They like you because you have maids back home.

They like you because you're a doctor there and a nurse's aide here.

They like you because you have a college degree they say is only the equivalent of a ninth-grade American education.

They like you because you can't fill out an application form.

They like you because you speak broken English, and always say, Yes.

They like you because you keep it all to yourself.

They like you because you take it in, all the way down.

They like you because you ask for it, adore it.

They like you because you're a copycat, want to be just like them.

They like you because—give it a few more years—you'll be just like them.

And when that time comes, will they like you more?

VENDETTA

Fuckin' witch. I hate that Jap. Who she think her? I cannot wait for crack her face. I hate you, Takemoto, I hate you so much, you just wait, you fuckin' momona bitch. No freakin' tell me for cool my jets, assholes. You shut up. So what if we passin' the church? Big fuckin' deal. Besides, you think deaf-eared Father Pacheco can hear us. Shit, he rather listen to confessions. Fuck you, Edgar, I ain't gettin' all hysterical. And if I am, you think I goin' be spendin' my freakin' energy on jerks like you. Shit, you guys supposed to be my friends and then. You guys know she always on my case ever since school started. No try shake your head, Florante, cuz she always razz you down come SRA and oral presentation time cuz of your Flip accent, so no make like I gettin' paranoid for nothin'. Worse part is she make like she all nice nice when she lecturin' me about my Maybellines, Danskins, tube-tops, and mini-skirts. "Oh, Trina dear, don't you think you should be wearing something more appropriate than a tube-top, especially since you spend the whole recess time playing Chinese jump rope," or, "Trina, today in civilization, there is a term to describe girls like you who flirt with older boys," or, "I do hope your mother knows the price she's paying for making a duplicate of herself." Need I say more? Duplicate, my ass. Dumb envious Jap, she hates my mother's guts so much. Like know why? Cuz my mother stay screwin' her husband. Mr. Takemoto, alias Uncle Craig. Mailman by day. Toshiro Mifune by night. For days, you guys. No act like you was born yesterday. Old news, already. Like know what else? My mother's three-months hapai. No kid you guys, brah. You really think I creative enough for make somethin' up like this? Yeah, three months, already. In fact, Uncle Craig just wen' take her OBGYN couple days ago, ultrasound, the whole works. No believe then, freakas. If I was lyin', you think that dried-up tuna goin' be throwin' temper tantrums each time I enter the class? Sad part is she can only take it out on me cuz if she ever try wise up to my mother, she never ever goin' teach in this world again. Problem with her is that she think I so stupid, always bitin' her dust, that I cannot catch what she tellin' the whole valley about me and my mother, which is us as cheap whores of Kalihi. But I ain't goin' sit on my ass and put up with her marital PMS. No freakin' way. Not anymore. Not after what she did to me this afternoon at Longs Drugs. I no can believe. I was so embarassed, so humiliated. More worse, I was with Erwin Castillo, OIA star quarterback. Between aisle nine and ten, Lay's potato chips and Hallmark cards, she wen' announce to all us Longs Drugs shoppers that I, Katherine Katrina-Trina Cruz, nothin' but one bastard, and my mother, one homewrecker. Urgh, I wanted for pound her face right there and then. I was so humiliated, and even more humiliated when I had to explain to Erwin what one bastard was. And he, he just gave me this funny kind look like, "Oh, gross, you no more one father?" How much you like bet? Yeah, he still wen' walk me home, but he was on the other side of the street. I like kill somebody already. So humiliated. If Erwin no invite me for go steady with him, or even just to his Winter Prom, cuz she told everybody in Longs Drugs I one bastard, that freakin' witch goin' get it. She goin' get it so bad, by the time it's over, she not goin' have her two sons for bring her flowers come Mother's Day.

Daldalera

—Katrina and her mother are a disgrace to the Filipino race.

—You think they'd be more civilized than those back in PI. Mabuti na lang I wasn't born here.

—Me also. But don't worry kasi they don't act like Filipinos. They can't even speak a word of Tagalog.

—Or Ilocano. Ay, mare, no matter how much they deny their Filipinoness, they're still Pinoys in the eyes of the Americans. And if the Americans said they're Americans, too, I'd pack up my bags and take the first flight back to PI.

—They should be locked up, with all this kabastusan they're doing.

—Or be sent back to PI where they'd learn a thing or two about discipline.

—At delikadesa, mare. I mean, what ten-year-old girl out there goes to school looking like a puta?

—That's because Katrina's mother would rather spend her time getting pregnant by a married man.

—Speaking of putas, mare, do you remember Mrs. Lord?

—The gold-digger Filipina who had five husbands?

—Yes.

—What about her?

—This past Saturday, I ran into her at the open market next to Kalakaua Intermediate—ay, mare, that market is much cheaper than Star Market atsaka fresh pa ang mga vegetables. Anyway, she said buntis daw si Katrina.

—Talaga? Siguro naman tsismis lang 'yan. You know naman how much Mrs. Lord loves to gossip.

—No, she said it's a fact daw.

—How can Katrina be pregnant, she's only ten years old?

—Trust me, mare. I may not believe much of what that gold-digger Visayan says, but I wouldn't doubt it if Katrina is pregnant because of the way she acts.

—And who's the father?

—Erwin Castillo.

—Erwin Castillo? Isn't he a football player?

—Correction, mare. He's not only a football player, he's the OIA Player of the Year.

—So this is another case of like mother, like daughter.

—Exactly.

—But pregnant or not pregnant, mare, I'm sorry to say that young as she is, I cannot give her my sympathy. I mean, if you only attended the Sunday mass, mare, you'd be so shocked. Can you imagine she and her mother go to church dressed up like prostitutes?

—Talaga?

—Really. Worse part is they come in fifteen minutes before the mass is about to end, right before Father Pacheco is about to begin communion. That's why he always gets his Lamb of God speech confused.

—And do they go up and take their communion?

—Not only that, mare. Right after they eat the body of Christ, they bring out their cosmetics and start painting their faces in front of everybody.

—How vulgar.

—And sometimes, when they sit beside me, and I listen to their conversation, all I hear coming out of their mouths is fack this, fack that. I tell you, if it weren't for my son, I would not go to church.

—By the way, how is he now?

—Salamat sa dios, cured na siya. We took him to the Rehab and he was there for six months. It was so painful, mare. But, thank God, it's all over now.

—Is he still a member of Da Manong Gang?

—Not anymore. Ikaw naman, how is your husband doing na? Is he out na ba?

—Five more years. I pray every night that they will give him probation soon kasi I cannot handle working and taking care of the three boys. Ay, naku, mare, change the subject na lang before my blood pressure goes up.

—I'm sorry, mare, I didn't know it was that terrible.

—It's okay.

—...

—...

—So what else did Mrs. Lord say?

—She also mentioned that the De Los Reyes family are leaving the valley

—But they just moved in less than a year ago, di ba?

—Yes. Pero, according to Mrs. Lord, it's because of their landlord Mr. Batongbacal.

—Bakit?

—Mrs. Lord said it's something about Mr. Batongbacal going to the hospital.

—Again?

—Yes. Lita drove him to Saint Francis last night.

—Why?

—I'm not really sure, pero I will call you once Mrs. Lord tells me.

—Sige.

—Ay, naku, mare, sometimes I wonder what will we ever talk about once these Filipinos leave our sight.

    —Which ones? The disgraceful ones or those about to fall from grace?

    —Both.

    —Siguro we'll finally have peace of mind, and a boring life.

    —That's so true, mare, so true.

You Don't
Have To Wait

You and your son Jeremy are hypnotized by Merv Griffin. Your wife is napping. Snap out of it, Mr. Batongbacal, you've got work to do. Summon her tubercular body out of the bedroom and into her car.

(Tell her, *Beer!* you've run out of beer) "Lita, drive to Star Market and get me a six-pack of Bud."

"I just got home."

(So) "So what? there's no beer left in the fridge. I want you to go to Star and get me my six-pack now, hurry, before..." (Before you lose your temper) "Before I lose my temper."

"But I'm tired."

(No) "No. When I tell you to do something I want you to do it. I don't care if you have to sleepwalk your way to get to the market. I want my beer and that's that."

She looks pissed and tired, but a man's got to do what a man's got to do. She sleepwalks out of the house and into the car. Switches on the ignition, presses the gas pedal, and she's off. One down, one to go.

Shut Merv Griffin up, and get rid of Jeremy, quick.

"Go to your room."

"But I want to watch the news."

(Late night news) "You can watch the news later on tonight. I want you to go to your room..." (Homework) "and do your homework."

"But it is part of my homework, Dad."

(He's got you)

"Mrs. Kashiwahara always gives us pop quizzes on current events."

(He's really got you)

"..."

"..."

(I got it, the clarinet! He hasn't been practicing that second-hand Bundy clarinet you bought him from Easy Music Store) "Where's the clarinet I bought you?"

"In my room."

"How come I haven't heard you play it lately?"

"Because..."

(Gotcha)

"Cuz..."

"Well, get your skinny ass in the room and don't come out until you can play..." (Gershwin backwards) "Gershwin backwards; you got me?"

"Cheeze wheeze, Dad. I didn't know you knew Gershwin."

(Smart-aleck) "Don't cheeze-wheeze-dad me, wise ass, or I'll kick your butt across the room."

Just a few seconds left. Go run to the bathroom, fix yourself up, but don't take too long.

My my, Mr. Batongbacal, you look slick. And gee, your hair smells terrific. Alberto VO5? Really? And your cologne, it's so musky. Wait, let me guess. Jovan? No? English Leather? No? I give up. Old Spice?! Could've fooled me.

Jing's turning from the corner. Quick, sprint to the floral drapes your wife recently purchased at the Kress 2-for-1 sale. This time, try to be inconspicuous. Do not stick your head out and grin from behind the curtain before Mrs. Freitas, who is watching you from her kitchen window, has a heart attack from seeing your gold-capped tooth, toupee, and fat eyebrows.

Oh, baby, check Jing out. Se-Xy! Brooke Shields, look out cuz nothing comes between Jing and her Chemin de Fer jeans, tube-tops, and thong sandals with the rings around the big toe.

"Good afternoon, Mrs. Freitas."

"Good afternoon, Jing."

She stops in front of two yellow-painted mailboxes and bends to scratch her knees.

"Freaking ants."

(You love it when she swears)

She opens the mailbox marked 1715-A, scans through the piles of letters, shakes her head. Bills, bills, and more bills, except for the brown envelope that says her mother has won another million dollars, and all she has to do is subscribe to five of the fifty thousand magazines of her choice from the long sheet of perforated stamps. Jing dumps it in the trash bin marked 1715-A.

She unlatches the gate that protects your one-story house with the three-bedroom extension your wife's family built eons ago. She scratches her knees again, then throws her nose in the air. Sniff, sniff, sniff. She smells something fishy. And it ain't Chicken of the Sea. She stops right below you, looks up into your eyes blossoming among the daisies.

"Fucking asshole."

Ignore her. She's had a rough day at school. Confrontation with Ms. Sugihara, who warned her that if her grades don't improve by next quarter, she can kiss her aerosplit and pom-poms goodbye. So have some sympathy for the poor cheerleader in distress.

What? Your throat's dry? Do you have any Halls? No? How about

Sucrets? No? What, Li Hing Mui seeds on the coffee table? Perfect. Go grab some. They're more fast-acting than Halls and you can sleep for hours tonight.

Feel better? Good. Is she still staring at you? Great. Spit the seed out, clear your throat, cross your fingers, spin three times, open the door, and, in your very best Tom Jones impersonation, invite her in.

"Good aaaafffternoon, JJJJing."

She gives you the Linda Blair look from *The Exorcist*.

(No need to wipe her sandals on the God Bless Our Home doormat your wife bought from the Arts & Crafts Fair at Thomas Square) "Do you wanna ccccome up and watch TV wwwwith Jeremy? You ddon't hhhhave to take off your saandals."

(Quit stuttering and offer her a drink) "Do you want some Kool-Aid?"

(No, not kiddie drink) "Or strawberry daiquiri, perhaps?"

(Something stronger) "How about orange juice and vodka?"

"How about taking a screw and driving it up your ass at the speed of light?"

Aw. Now, Mr. Batongbacal, control your temper. Pretend you didn't hear her. Now, now, lighten up. She's said worse things before. Besides, it's not worth getting all huffy-puffy about. It'll add more wrinkles on your face, and you've already got enough lines to start a Tic-Tac-Toe game-a-thon.

It's not that you're not attractive. You look much more appealing than Lawrence Welk. That's for sure. And of course you shouldn't hold your anger in. Go vent it out. Go pound on Jeremy's door.

(Tell him he can't play for shit) "Jeremy, quit tooting that fucking thing. You can't play for shit. (Bass drum, tuba) You should've just stuck to bass drum or tuba."

He doesn't hear you. "Open the fucking door, Jeremy, before I break it down."

He still doesn't hear you. So go ahead, kick the damn thing.

"What's the matter, Dad?"

Give him a couple of hard slaps in the head.

"You stupid fag, didn't you hear me knocking?"

Slap him in the face, too, while you're at it.

"I'm sorry, Dad."

"Sorry what?"

"Sorry, Daddie Dearest."

Is his face red? Good. Now, tell him to stop all that nonsense about current events pop quizzes and becoming the next Benny Goodman before he finds his head inside *The CBS Evening News With Walter Cronkite*.

It's almost five-thirty. Put on your invisible badge and march down to the back of the house, the extension your wife inherited from her grand-mother. Circle the house and stop where the bathroom is. Don't whistle or hum, or you won't get a backstage pass. Double-check your watch and make sure you're not too early, or else you'll only end up with Bino.

Is it five-thirty? Are you sure? Shhh, here she comes. Go ahead. Press your face against the screen, but don't press too hard or the screen will snap and you'll have to drive to City Mill to replace it first thing in the morning.

What? She's stepping into the shower with clothes on? Are you sure? Are you positively sure? Darn it. Don't worry, patience is a virtue. And like the good book says, great things always happen in the end as long as you slow your breathing down.

Mr. Batongbacal? Hello? Wake up and smell the Folgers, Mr. Batong-bacal; that's the shower you're hearing. If you want to whistle, this is the best time.

So, how did your day go? Nothing much? Want to hear a joke? What do you call Portuguese guys fighting in a car? Cabral. Get it, car brawl. How about a knock-knock? Knock knock. Who's there? Boo-hoo. Boo-hoo who? Why are you crying, Mr. Batongbacal?

What's taking her so long? The water has stopped running for minutes now. Don't get all excited, Mr. Batongbacal. Shhh, she's coming out. Shit, she heard you. Back off, Mr. Batongbacal. Away from the screen, damn it, before she snatches the giant can of Raid and wastes it all on your face, like she did the last time and your wife had to rush you to Saint Francis.

Gee, that was a close call. Now, now, Mr. Batongbacal. Don't get all hysterical. Besides, remember your motto: Once you've seen one, you've seen 'em all.

Go home. It's dinner time. Go and have your little *Brady Bunch* dinner. Hang out with the Missus and Jeremy. Watch *Three's Company* and *The Ropers*. Or suggest a board game. Clue sounds good. But not those heart-attack games like Operation or Super Perfection.

Ooops, it's nearing eight o'clock. Say goodnight to Jeremy.
"'Night 'night, Jeremy."
(How cute. Now apologize to him about this afternoon)
"Hey, Jeremy, I'm really sorry about what happened this afternoon."
"It's okay, Dad."
Now say night-night to Missus. Tuck her in bed if you're feeling up to it. No? All right, it was just a suggestion.
"Good night, honey."

It's eight o'clock, pitch-black. Put on your invisible badge and tiptoe out of the house. Watch your step. Are you standing by the malunggay tree overlooking Jing's bedroom? Then what are you waiting for? Stretch out your claws and jump that tree. Not so loud. Stop shaking or all the leaves will fall and there'll be nothing to make that chicken kalamungay soup with. And be careful because the branch is not that sturdy. It might snap, and they'll have to cast up your legs again. Stay still. Shhh. And quit that heavy breathing. Everyone in the house can hear you. You don't want to spend the rest of the evening with Mr. and Mrs. Stanley Roper now, do you? Well, be quiet then.

What time is it? Eight-fifteen? Are you positive? Oh, you're wearing the watch that glows in the dark? My, my, we are prepared tonight. Just don't get carried away or you'll forget about the eight-thirty deadline when Auntie Marlene pulls into the garage to drop off Jing's mother from her night class. But don't worry, that's fifteen minutes from now.

So what is Jing wearing? A pink nightshirt? Does it have a picture of a pony or a little girl wearing a beanie cap? A girl? That's Strawberry Shortcake. Bino gave it to her for Christmas.

Mr. Batongbacal? Mr. Batongbacal? Hello. Earth calling Mr. Batongbacal. What is she doing? Thumbing through *Tiger Beat* or *16* magazine? No? Is she brushing her hair in front of the dresser mirror? No? Trying on perfume? Jontue? Charlie? White Linen? Prince Matchabelli? Yes. Hmmmmm. Stop and smell the air. Makes you want to walk through her bedroom wall, huh? Run your fingers through her hair, sample the perfume on her skin. Closer, Mr. Batongbacal. Come closer... Oh well, time's up. Sorry. Now, hold your breath, tighten up those ligaments, and one, two, three, jump. Don't look so sad, Mr. Batongbacal. Run to the bathroom, lock the door, turn on the shower, let it all out. It only takes the thought of her and a couple of jerks. Don't forget to wash up. Cleanliness is next to Godliness.

What? You can't wait til tomorrow? Nor can I, Mr. Batongbacal, and you know why? So I can tell the entire valley to wear their invisible badges and come here to this yard. Their eyes will bug out when they see your Mr. Cleanliness body trying to balance on the branch. Oh no, Mr. Batongbacal, don't worry about them shaking the tree. They won't need to. All they have to do is whistle for the branch to snap. You'll fall flat on your fat face and break all your bones. And Jing will have nothing to do with it, because by the time you come back, all cast-up and wearing your shower cap, she and her family will be gone. Yes, Mr. Batongbacal, gone.

What Manong Rocky Tells Manang Pearly About Carmen, Rosario, And Milagros

Eh, how many times I wen' tell you stay away from those three sisters? You deaf or what? Like me clean your ears with one broom? You better watch it cuz the next time I catch you near them, I not goin' regret whatever I goin' do to you. No, no try open your mouth, no try explain, cuz I saw you, stupid. You think I blind? I not blind. I think you the one blind. I was drivin' by and I saw you talkin' to them in front Kalihi-Uka School, so no lie to me before I give you one slap in the head. Maybe that's what you need, ah? Maybe one good slap goin' finally put some sense into your stupid head.

Look at that house, that glass house they go around braggin' to everybody that they, and not their husbands, was the ones who wen' pour blood, sweat, and tears. Blood, sweat, and tears, my ass. Maybe was them the one who had the money, but was their husbands who wen' bust their ass buildin' it. If it wasn't for them, those wahines goin' still be livin' in that grass shack. Who they think them, anyway, buildin' one glass house way on top the mountain? They no more shame or what? Everybody can see what they doin'. Tommy said one time, he wen' watch Mila watch her husband vacuum for eternity and all she did was sit on her lazy ass and chain-smoke cigarettes.

What? What you mean how can Tommy see that close when he lives all the way by the cemetery? Maybe he was usin' his binoculars or somethin'. Shit, I don't know. I no ask him that kind personal stuff. Why you like know for, anyway? That's his business, not yours. Oh, just sharrup and go get me my beer in the fridge.

I tell you, everytime I pass Murphy Street, I like walk up that hill and break that house down, and false crack their husbands, too, for doin' all that housework shit. They piss me off. They piss us guys off. We already wen' warn 'em many times before, we told 'em, "Eh, braddahs, you guys know what you gettin' yourselves into or what? Think hard now, no act irrational, no get sucked by their pretty faces cuz beauty only stay skin deep." But what do those guys do after our man-to-man talk? What do those pussywhip haoles do?

Even Father Pacheco tried to talk them out of it. Eh, no say that. That priest might only care for his red wine and church donations, too, but he get one big heart and he just like one prophet when he stay sober. He knew way aheada time what they goin' end up doin' if they marry those sisters. He sensed it cuz he knows those wahines like they was his own daughters. Boy, did he hit the bull's-eye. Oh, sharrup. I said no talk like that about Father Pacheco. Sharrup, I said. You talk too much. Why no make yourself useful for once and go get my packa cigarettes in my shirt pocket. Hurry up.

Eh, stupid woman, you come bring me my cigarettes but where's the lighter? What you expect me to light my cigs with? My fuckin' fingers?

Sit your ass down and tell me what you was doin' talkin' to those witches in front the school? Yeah, that's right, they nothin' but witches. And I get proof, too. Tommy told me that Roberto wen' tell him that one night, while he and Nolan and a buncha other guys was comin' down from the mountain from hunting wild pigs, they wen' spot three women that wen' look just like Carmen, Rose, and Mila. "Had to be them, brah," Roberto wen' tell Tommy. "They was dancin' and screamin' and just like they was speakin' in tongues." Then Tommy told me that Roberto wen' tell him that alla sudden, one of 'em wen' take off her clothes and started rollin' around on the dirt.

Of course, I believe Roberto. Of course, could only be those sisters, cuz, tell me, what women crazy enough for be runnin' around naked and wild in the mountain, and at night? You? Thought so. Shit, all this talk makin' me thirsty. Go get me one 'nother beer.

Why you so quiet alla sudden? Got you all shook up? So, how come you still never answer my question? I said what they was tellin' you in front the school? That they Filipinas and goin' prove to you by speakin' fluent Tagalog? Big fuckin' deal. I could care less if they speak fluent Spanish. I bet they was talkin' stink about me, ah? No shake your head. No make like you was born yesterday. Shit, you can lie better than that. Recipes, my ass. They no even cook, let alone do the grocery. How I know? Cuz Tommy wen' tell me so, that's how.

What? They wen' invite you over their house for dinner? For what? So they can feed you more horseshit about me, ah, like they wen' do to Elwood's wife Marianne? Shit, they was probably the one who wen' tell Marianne that Elwood was foolin' around with Thelma. What you mean Marianne already knew about Elwood and Thelma way before she went over to Mila's them place for dinner? No, that's fulla shit cuz only us guys knew about Elwood and Thelma, and real guys no squeal on their friends.

'Sides, if Marianne wen' suspect that Elwood and Thelma was already foolin' around, then how come she only waited for that night, that night she had dinner with Mila and Rose them, to shoot Elwood's balls to thy kingdom come?

Shit, I not goin' be surprised if they already wen' poison your mind by tellin' you that I already screwin' somebody else cuz I been comin' home early in the mornin'. I just like remind you that that's cuz I busy lookin' for one job. So what if Elwood was unemployed when he was humpin' Thelma? That no mean that I goin' be humpin' Thelma, too. If ever I goin' screw around, not goin' be with Thelma, that's for sure. Elwood was stupid from the start. He had to choose his next-door neighbor to hump. Not me, no ways. I goin' go for the kill. I goin' find somebody young, somebody real pretty and rich, too, so I no gotta bust my ass lookin' for jobs. And I guarantee you, she not goin' be somebody like Thelma who look like she wen' live through three world wars.

What you cryin' for? Come over here. Come here, I said. I promise I not goin' hurt you. I hate it when you start cryin' for nothin'. Eh, all I askin' is for you not to mingle with those sisters, cuz they bad news, babe. You think they care about you? Look what happened to Marianne. She went nuts after the shooting, but did they ever visit her at Kaneohe Hospital? Shit, no. And for them to be tellin' you they Filipinas just pisses me off to the max. You should know that.

Try compare yourself to them. You work two jobs, they only get one. You cook, garden, go Star Market, they don't. You memorize which aisles Brut, Mr. Clean, and Tide are in. You get 'em downpacked, babe. And you, you the only one of the few in the valley who knows that patis, shoyu, and jar of bagoong only go on sale at BC Market. You yourself said so, right? On top of that, you one mother. But them, they don't know jackshit.

So tell me, who get the advantage in the end? You or them? You, of course. You somebody, one wife, one mother, superwoman. But them, they nothin'. All they get is a buncha losers for husbands who walk around pretendin' they no mind cookin' and cleanin' and bein' bossed around. If you still no catch the picture, I goin' paint 'em for you one more time. They like destroy us, you, me, our daughter Rowena, and everythin' that's special between us three. That's why they like get you into their side of the yard. Right now, they makin' you think you this, you that, one nobody, but the moment you believe all that rubbish, I tell you, babe, nobody goin' give a damn about you. And I mean nobody. Not them, not your parents, your brothers, your daughter. And especially, not me. You better believe it, babe. So come over here and give me a kiss.

IN THE NAME OF
THE MOTHER

Manong Rocky is at it again, turning the living room upside down and inside out because he can't find the plastic bag that keeps him awake for days, and sometimes weeks.

"And energetic, brah, no forget energetic," he says, though energy is the last thing to cross people's minds when they see his skinny body sprawled on the porch with his eyes staring out into space.

He enters the bedroom, which is fully made up like a honeymoon suite, and goes straight for the closet. He slides the closet door open and begins searching for the Ziploc bag among the neatly pressed clothes. One by one he inspects each and every garment, feeling the pockets and digging his hand in. Halfway through the rack, he starts pulling the clothes off the plastic hangers and flinging them across the room, tearing the straps of dresses.

He reaches for the old boxes on top of the closet shelf and dumps their contents on the floor. He rummages through documents, family photo albums, and memorabilia, but comes up empty-handed. Frustrated, he yanks out the vanity drawers, frantically hunting for the glass pipe and the powder that he insists keeps him going and going.

"Where the hell she wen put 'em?" he screams as he flips open the lid of the jewelry box, which, a few weeks ago, contained his wife's engagement ring, a pearl necklace, a diamond wedding ring, and a pair of sapphire earrings handed down to her from her great-grandmother. He trashes the entire vanity top, hurling perfume bottles, makeup kits, and a heart-shaped picture frame of their only daughter Rowena across the room.

He retreats to the living room and sits on the upholstered couch from

Wigwam Furniture Company. He pounds the coffee table, causing half-empty cans of beer and a bowl of leftover cereal to spill onto the stained carpet.

He gets up, walks into the kitchen, and starts tossing the canned goods onto the floor. He shoves his hand into an open box of Western Family baking soda, then sticks his forefinger into his mouth and sucks the powder until his teeth dig into skin. With blood trailing down his chin, he pitches the box across the room, hitting the bookshelf. "Fuckin' Pearly, you goin' get it," he screams.

The first—and only—time Manang Pearly hid the Ziploc bag from Manong Rocky, everyone in Hawai'i found out, courtesy of the morning and evening newspapers, the five local TV stations, a morning radio program, and COMAAH, or Coalition of Mothers Against Abusive Husbands.

She was so badly beaten she needed forty-eight stitches and three surgeries to align her spine, remove a ruptured spleen, and extract shards of beer mug glass from her face. She coded three times, had five blood transfusions, was tested for everything, and was given a toxic screen to see if she had been under the influence of alcohol or drugs.

She was seen by a dozen or so consultants, including a psychiatric resident who asked her if she or any members in her family had a history of mental illnesses. None. A hospital chaplain visited her room each noon and again at six o'clock to recite the Angelus. Between the consultations and prayers, she was wheeled to the Rehabilitation Unit where she spent a half hour learning how to move her upper and lower extremities, and another half hour learning how to say Wee-na, her daughter's nickname.

For weeks, readers found her making headlines in Section A of both *The Bulletin* and the *Inquirer*. SPOUSE ABUSE HITS ISLAND AGAIN. HUSBAND NEARLY BEATS WIFE TO DEATH. THIRD THIS YEAR BY

FILIPINO. Listeners tuned in to Kimo & Kawika on P-39 AM to keep abreast of her condition, as well as to voice their opinions and concerns regarding the issue. Viewers watched the local evening news, where each station devoted five-minute segments to her, Manong Rocky, and their daughter Rowena. KRTV even treated Rowena to all-you-can-eat ice cream at Farrell's after she spilled her guts in front of the camera.

Morning, noon, and night, Manang Pearly was the topic of current events pop quizzes, school papers, dissertations, and gossip. Diners, both young and old, talked of her victimization and passed it around the table as if it were salt and pepper. Sympathizers throughout the island sent her gifts, food baskets, money, and toys for Rowena, along with letters which spelled out "sorry," "support," "hope," and "victim."

On the day of her discharge, local residents and tourists trekked to Monte Street in Kalihi-Uka to catch a glimpse of the person who had so affected the lives of both Filipina and non-Filipina women. To them, she was a survivor and a victim, a saint and an idiot. Members of COMAAH camped out at the top of the street next to the grotto of the Virgin Mary the night before. She was, as *The Bulletin* put it, the biggest news to hit the island since the bombing of Pearl Harbor.

As the Oldsmobile veered onto Monte Street, she peered out the window and saw a mob of people turning her front yard into a battlefield. Reporters, journalists, and militant members of COMAAH rushed to the car being driven by an off-duty policeman, each of them dying to know if she had changed her mind and would press charges against her husband. "No," she said, "we have a daughter, and I don't want to break a holy vow."

The Purple Man
And His Disciples

JESUS OF KAM SHOPPING CENTER

Edgar christens him Jesus because he resembles the Jesus Christ molded into the bronze plaques hanging on the grey walls of Our Lady of the Mount church. Except Jesus of the Kam Shopping Center fame has an unruly beard, plaque teeth, hair like a doormat, black fingernails, and a gaze that spells "Resurrection." Or, "Terror."

He doesn't talk to anyone. Only to himself. Mumbles from one end of the lot to the other. About taxes. "I gotta pay my taxes or else they'll put me in prison, this world is one big prison, you know, I know it is, so is life, go home and set your alarm clock, my cousin went to prison in Oberlin, but before that he was living in Palo Alto, do you know where Oberlin is?" Then he rushes to a corner, curls himself up into a ball, and shrieks at the shoppers entering and exiting the automatic doors of Star Market or Longs Drugs.

He doesn't communicate with the Happy Face Man, Tutu Man, the Exorcist Lady, Irma the TNT Victim, Da Guy Ferdinand, or the Purple Man. They see each other every day, yet no words between them. "They're just like black ants," Florante says, "no sense of geography."

Once, Jesus and Tutu Man almost exchanged words with each other. They ran from the opposite ends of the mini-mall and converged in front of Kress, as if they were being pulled by a magnet. Jesus held out his arms, but Tutu Man panicked and fled to Fashion Fabrics.

Katrina thinks Jesus is suffering from paranoid schizophrenia. That's what it says in her book *The Race for a Cure: Schizophrenia and Other Mental Disorders*, the book she says she bought because of her fascination with Sally Field as Sybil.

"Maybe he talk to himself cuz got no other people to talk to," Loata says.

"Cuz maybe he is God," Edgar says.

"Maybe," Vicente says. "Maybe."

THE HAPPY FACE MAN

The Happy Face Man relies on the five trash bins spread out across Kam Shopping Center for his meals. Loata calls him the Happy Face Man because he looks like the Happy Face teachers draw on student's assignments. Button eyes and the wide arc of a smile that stretches all the way to the earlobes. Happy Face for "EXCELLENT." Or "VG" for "Very Good."

"You no think he kinda look like Pat Morita?" Loata asks.

"Who?" Vicente asks.

"Pat Morita, the guy who play Arnold in *Happy Days*."

"Yeah, he does," Katrina says, "except Pat Morita is bald and the Happy Face Man get stiff Rapunzel hair."

"Maybe he his lost younger brother," Edgar says.

"Maybe," Loata and Vicente say.

They watch him journey from one tan-colored trash bin painted with the phrase LEND A HAND TO CLEAN OUR LAND to the next, until he stops at the bin in front of Kenny's Burger House, his knee-length Brillo hair hiding his back.

"Hey, Happy Face Man," Loata shouts, "you Pat Morita's brother?"

No answer.

"Hey, Happy Face Man, I talkin' to you," Loata says.

"He no can hear you, dummy," Katrina says. "He schizophrenic, that's why. Like Jesus and Sybil. He only hear voices in his head."

Too many voices in one head. In one tongue. They fill his head until it's the size of a balloon, then POP! His tongue starts rolling at an uncontrollable speed, as if bitten by an invisible empire of red ants.

The Happy Face Man reappears from the trash bin, devouring leftover teriyaki beef.

Something flies out of his mouth, falls near his feet. He picks it up, puts it back in his mouth.

"Look," Edgar says, "he got Martha Raye in his mouth."

"Gross," Katrina says.

The Happy Face Man smiles wide, flashing a set of dentures more colorful than the rainbow.

TUTU MAN

Is hip. Red Danskins and cork sandals.

Is cool. Pink turban and a swan's neck.

Is futuristic. Plastic heart-shaped sunglasses and doorknob earrings.

Is what you get if you no come out of the closet, Edgar says.

Is the way he is cuz he don't know what he is, Katrina says.

Is Mr. Tourret ticking on his skin without an advance notice.

Is a smeared lipstick.

Across a muscle of lies.

Is cracking up on a cracked stone bench.

Is crossing his legs.

A laughing hyena.

Is crossing his legs tight.

Is crying out his brains.

THE EXORCIST LADY

From a distance, the Exorcist Lady, also known as Lily from Montana, seems pleasant and amicable. A middle-aged white woman, five feet tall, and red-haired, though Edgar presumes it's dyed since no one in Kalihi, not even the haoles, have red for hair.

Step a little closer and you'll see a bookbag clamped between her legs. Books by Judith Rossner, D.H. Lawrence, and Erica Jong, and a dozen or so *Playgirl* magazines.

The Exorcist Lady is notorious for smelling men of overflowing virility from miles away. Once her sensory organs start to work, she tracks her hope-to-be/soon-to-be coital partner.

"Eh, handsome, you wanna fuck me?" (her eyes big and lit), "unwrap your salami and let me take a bite of it" (her mouth wide, foaming at the corners), "squeeze my big tits" (hands over breasts, massaging), "I am hungry" (moans), "let me touch it, feel it, suck it..."

All men are afraid of her, turn into scaredy-cats and meow themselves to the highest trees. This excites Lily from Montana, who chases after them.

"Fuck me" (she screams), "hey, handsome man" (her eyes changing from blue to green), "fuck me, please" (legs spreading out like a gate), "fuck me, please" (voice shifting from alto to guttural), "I said fuck me" (until it sounds like a record spinning on a dying phonograph), "please, fa-aah-aaa..."

Once, she ran into Father Pacheco as he was walking out of Star Market with a bottle of red wine. She knelt to kiss his hand, then began trellising herself around his thighs and shoulders.

"Good morning, Father Pacheco," then: "You fuckin' cocksuckin' child molester," then: "When can I come for confession, Father?" then: "tonguing and fingering their tight buttholes why don't you come suck my tits?"

Climbing up to his mouth, she said, "Oh, Father, Father, suck my tits" (his eyes big and lit). "C'mon Father, please, Father..." (his eyes rolling once, twice).

Father Pacheco tried to free himself from her grasp. He pushed at her with his left hand and grabbed a naked titty. "Suck it, Father, so handsome for Jesus," she said, and the bottle of red wine fell from his right hand and smashed against the concrete.

Like Houdini or a contortionist, Father Pacheco chicken-winged his arms into his body and then drilled his elbows into her, turning out of her grasp.

"Puta! Hija de Satanas!" he shouted, taking a plastic bottle from his pocket and splashing holy water on Lily, who, tit still bare, aimed herself at a man in shorts exiting Star Market.

"What's her trip?" Loata asks.

"She one exhibitionist plus she get Mr. Coprolalia Syndrome," Katrina says.

"What's that?" Loata asks.

"That's when you get possessed by this man who get the power for make your mind all horny and your body all hungry," Katrina explains.

"Like Irma?" Vicente asks.

"No, but the opposite," Katrina says. "Irma stay like that cuz she married to Mr. Miller."

IRMA, THE TNT LADY

Irma Manlapit Miller. Tago nang tago. Always hiding from Mr. Miller of Kalihi Street. She can't stand it anymore. Day and night, in the shower, under the dining table, while cooking or sleeping, cramps or no cramps, whenever and wherever, he's at it. Banging her with his fifty-year-old sex machine that never shuts down because it doesn't run on 4-D batteries.

That's not all. For lunch hour he brings his friends, young and old, married or single, to his home and feeds them Irma tied up to the bedpost, blindfolded, gagged. He takes the first bite while the others wax their wings and flock around the room, waiting to peck on Irma.

She has no one to blame except her natural curls, permanently tanned skin, a cheap foundation her mother mopped on her face, a Polaroid Instamatic, and page ten of a catalog. She always hated having her picture taken, found it boring. But her mother was behind the photographer, cussing and threatening her to smile *beeg,* or else, or else.... She smiled bigger than *beeg*, and a registered parcel and a few months later, she was praying to Mama Mary on a plane bound for Hawai'i.

Dusk or dawn, rain or shine, she's throwing herself in front of moving cars slowly exiting the lot of Kam Shopping Center, or begging the shoppers on hands and knees in stammering Tagalog-English. *Pleez, Sir, Mum, maawa naman po kayo. Only por today, pleez, Sir, Mum. I'm a good person naman e. Jus deez once. Puwede pleez.* Yes or no. Meal or no meal, she'll be deeply grateful. *Salamat very much po. God bless you po.* For the blanket and the little corner in a garage where she can lie on a bed of old newspapers and watch out for the one-eyed Kalihi Valley bug with a ten-inch antenna.

Irma Manlapit Miller. Tago nang tago. Searching for Manila at the rainbow end of an oil slick, and thinking how foolish she was to let her mother sell her bigger than *beeg* smile for a blue book, an eagle stamp, a ten-hour flight to Mr. Miller of 3123 Kalihi Street who always tracks her down, drags her home, and mounts her high on his bedroom wall.

DA GUY FERDINAND

Is christened by Florante because he acts just like Ferdinand Magellan, but in a Kalihi scale. Always insisting he's the protector of Summer Theaters located between Longs Drugs and Silver Dragon.

"Without me," he boasts, "you Filipinos would have no Tagalog movies to watch."

"Screw you, Ferdinand," Edgar shouts.

"No, my little mestizo son, I am the reason why Tagalog movies are still shown here at Kam Shopping Center."

"How?" Katrina asks.

"By speaking to the President of Summer Theaters. I convinced him that if he wants to be rich he must show Tagalog movies because Filipinos, though they speak English, don't understand English."

"Up yours," Katrina shouts.

"Calm down, my beautiful child, calm down. This is nothing to be angry about. I'm only doing it for your benefit."

"What benefit?" Florante asks.

"Last night I had a vision, one that prompted me to speak to the President of Summer Theaters. I told him that with all the money he's earning from showing Tagalog movies here in Hawai'i, he should buy a mini-film studio in Manila and make his own Tagalog movies because Filipinos there would kill for money. And they'd also kill to be in the movies."

"You talkin' bubbles," Katrina says.

"And by God, he saw it. I made him see it. And he said to me, 'Ferdinand, you are a genius.' I smiled and told him, 'I know I know.' You, too, kids. You, too, can be rich like the President of Summer Theaters. All you have to do is save some money, go to the Philippines, and open up your own film studios. But make sure you tell your people that you are helping them, not using them, that you are laughing with them, not at them. Now, aren't you going to thank me because I'm such a wonderful genius?"

"Please, Minerva," Edgar says. "If you so smart, how come you talkin' through your ass?"

"Talking through my what?" Ferdinand asks.

"Through your colonial colon," Florante answers.

"My genius what?" Ferdinand asks.

"Your colonial colon that should've been removed centuries ago," Florante says.

THE PURPLE MAN

"Oh, oh," Loata shouts. "The Purple Man, look, the Purple Man." Who lives on Gulick Street. In a purple house with a purple fence, purple mailbox, three purple trash cans, purple garage.

"Is he really a pimp?" Vicente asks.

"Yeah," Loata replies. "My uncle's co-worker's cousin's aunt say he pimp his wife all the time. And she also say that when you see his purple car comin', you better run for your life cuz he goin' turn you into one prostitute."

"He not one pimp," Katrina says. "He just crazy, that's all. Pupule to the max. From wearin' all that purple. Purple pants, purple shirt, purple shoes, purple socks, purple visor, purple shades."

"He not crazy crazy," Edgar says. "He just kinda slow cuz my father's calabash cousin's cousin, Uncle Charlie, he say he stay like that cuz he got boxed in the head too many times. He say the Purple Man used to be one heavyweight champ long, long time ago. Before Muhammad Ali and Andy Ganigan."

"What is he anyway?" Vicente asks.

"Haole," Loata says.

"Hawaiian," Katrina says.

"Filipino," Edgar says.

All at the same time.

"How much you like bet he Hawaiian?" Katrina asks.

"A million bucks he Filipino," Edgar says.

"A Happy Meal he one haole," Loata says.

The Purple Man drives his purple bug from the opposite end of the mall. The bug passes by Star Market, and shoppers pushing grocery-filled carts stop at once, their faces blank, eyes unblinking. He parks in front of Pete's Modelcraft, and its automatic doors lose their magnetic sensories. The purple engine shuts off and all signs of movement freeze. As if the Purple Man owns the key to the world and has just turned it off.

He opens the car door, whistling "Purple Haze." Tutu Man, who flees from Jesus, halts the second he passes the Purple Man.

"Let's go," Vicente says. "He's coming towards us."

"Too late," Katrina says.

"Just stay, Vicente," Loata says. "He not goin' hurt you."

"'Sides," Edgar says, "you no can run away from the Purple Man."

"Why? What do you mean I can't run away from him?" Vicente asks, his voice trembling.

"Shit, Vicente," Edgar says. "This not the right time for get all anxiety up. Everythin' just goin' look purple, that's all."

"But no worry," Loata adds. "The thing not goin' last long."

"Yeah," Katrina says. "Goin' look just like you swimmin' by one octopus and all of a sudden the octopus squeeze out all this ink for make the water all cloudy."

KALIHI IS IN
THE HEART
The #7 green bus that rattles in and
out of Kalihi Valley looks as if it's been salvaged from a junkyard with its
rusty sides, hard seats, and tightly shut windows that could only be
opened by the muscles of an Arnold Schwarzenegger.

"Ridin' that bus make me feel like I re-livin' the freakin' plantation
days," Katrina says. "All I need when I in that bus is one cane knife and
the picture goin' be perfect."

"I know, yeah, so hot in there, I feel like I in one sauna," Edgar says.
"Only thing missin' for make my bus ride picture come perfect is Scott
sweatin' beside me."

When the doors of the green bus squeak open to invite Edgar for a
hot ride, he makes sure that he's brought his First Aid Kit: His blue duffel bag carrying two T-shirts, a bottle of ice-cold water, a face towel, magazines, Jordache sunglasses, magic markers, and Bain de Soleil.

While the others roast on wooden seats, Edgar gives himself a Por-
tuguese sponge bath, which lasts for ninety seconds, before he applies the
suntan lotion. To maintain freshness, he fans his face with back issues of
Boys' Life or *GQ;* to keep himself breathing, Vicks Inhaler; and to preoc-
cupy and prevent himself from fainting, he flips through *Tiger Beat* or
Dynamite magazines, or he magic markers the seats to tell the rest of
Kalihi that E&S WUZ HEA. E for Edgar, and S for Scott, as in Scott
Baio.

◆

For only a dime—twenty-five cents for high school graduates and over—the #7 green bus offers a passenger an hour's tour around Kalihi: Kam Shopping Center, the open market between Kalakaua Intermediate and Kalihi-Kai, Libby's Manapua Shop, Asagi Hatchery, Puuhale School, Dillingham Prison, Puuhale Market, Warren's Store, the Purple Man's house on Gulick, and the projects named after Hawaiian kings and princes, like King Kamehameha Housing, King Kamehameha IV Housing, and Prince Kuhio Park Terrace.

◆

One afternoon, a deaf-and-dumb couple visiting from Orange County, California was on their way to pay tribute to the drowned souls of the USS Arizona. By accident, they got off on Dillingham Street and transferred to the unventilated green bus, clutching their bags.

The bus was jammed with passengers, mostly students and hotel workers in their hotel uniforms. After three bus stops, the woman signed to her husband to tell him she was having an asthma attack: Worse: Than: Pago: Pago. She signed off before the paramedics arrived. Her husband fainted then DOA'd at Queen's Hospital.

The tragedy reached their son, a very powerful and conservative Republican who served in the Nixon Administration. He sent a telegram to Bob Matayoshi, the Councilman for the Kalihi district, who was busy preparing for his '78 Wanna-Job-Vote-For-Bob gubernatorial speech. The telegram read: Will be there...Be prepared...Your ass...Grass. An hour later, Councilman Matayoshi was rushed to Kuakini hospital with uncontrollable palpitations. He had an angina the size of a fist, then RIP'd at the age of thirty-nine.

◆

It's only the green bus that makes it's home in Kalihi, not the yellow, air-conditioned one that is striped with orange-and-black and has leather-upholstered seats. The yellow bus is for tourists wearing Noxema on their Rudolphs, Polaroid shades, and plastic colored visors, and shouldering complimentary airline bags packed with films, flyers for discount meals and group tickets to see the SOS band perform at the Outrigger Show-room. Dinner includes two complimentary drinks, but not the latest SOS cassette tape that comes with a free autographed poster of the band known for its versatility and sequins.

Like a spaceship on wheels, the yellow bus flies from Waikiki and Ala Moana to: 1) the USS Arizona that looks like MacArthur's dentures float-ing in Pearl Harbor; 2) the long stretches of pineapple fields in Whitmore Village, Wahiawa; 3) the sugar plantation in Waialua; or 4) Sea Life Park where Flipper's understudies live.

◆

Except for the Bishop Museum and the Planetarium, Kalihi is not listed in *Places To Visit In Oahu*.

"Every time I pass by all those tourists waitin' for go inside Bishop Museum," Katrina says, "I like break their line and tell 'em, 'Eh, you guys blind or what? When come to old and dead stuffs, your eyes bulge out, but when come to me, you guys pretend for be blind.'"

"Cuz to them, you invisible," Edgar says. "But to you, they not."

"I no catch, Edgar," Loata says.

"Dumbass, close your eyes and pretend you one tourist in Kalihi. What you see?"

Eyes closed, Loata begins to map out Kalihi. "Get Kam Shopping Center, the open market, Higa's store, Boulevard Saimin, Fujiya's Ink, Sato's Shave Ice Store, the Purple Man's house, Pohaku's Bar...."

"Dumbass, that's all local places you seein', not tourist traps," Edgar interrupts.

"What else he supposed to see, smartass?" Katrina jumps in.

"You guys not gettin' the whole picture," Edgar says. "What's right next to Bishop Museum and the Planetarium?"

"Kalihi-Palama Library and the freeway," Loata says.

"Edgar, I not blind," Katrina says. "I pass the museum and cross that manini overpass every day when I go Farrington High for meet Erwin."

"If you not blind, then tell me what you see," Edgar says.

Katrina shuts her eyes and taps her fingers on her temples. "Get the museum, the planetarium, the library, the freeway, then Farrington High...."

"Hurry up, Trina, I no more all day," Edgar says.

"Wait, it's comin'," she says.

Lightbulb opens her eyes. She grins at Edgar. "Ohhhhh, I get it."

"What?" Loata says.

Edgar clears his throat, then signals Loata to applaud. "Welcome back to the 25th Annual Ms. Kalihi Universe 1979. I'm your host, Bob Barker," he says, holding an invisible microphone to his mouth. "And now I'm going to ask our tenth and final contestant Ms. Cruz to please come on down."

Katrina sashays to Edgar.

"Ms. Katherine Katrina-Trina Cruz, if you are to become Ms. Kalihi 1979, what is the first thing you are going to change in Kalihi?" Edgar asks.

Katrina takes the invisible microphone from Edgar's hand. "If I'm chosen Ms. Kalihi 1979, the first thing I'm going to do is move the freakin' freeway away from the Bishop Museum and the Planetarium so the tourists no can make one quick getaway to Waikiki, thank you," Katrina says, smiling wide.

"Why?" Loata interrupts, still confused.

"Dumbass, you think the tourists goin' like go wanderin' around Kalihi?" Katrina snaps.

"They no gotta go wanderin' around," Loata says. "They can just walk to Kam Shopping Center from Bishop Museum."

"And what? Freak out when they run into Tutu Man or the Purple Man?" Katrina asks.

"You no remember what wen' happen to the Orange County couple or what?" Katrina asks.

"Yeah, I do," Loata says. "The wife wen' have one heart attack and the husband wen' die right after that, but that's cuz they was ridin' the green bus and they no could breathe."

"For your information, Loata, she never had one heart attack. She had one attack of Asthmatic Claustrophobia," Edgar says.

"Asthmatic what?" Loata says.

"Not Asthmatic Claustrophobia, Edgar, but Asthmatic Otraphobia," Katrina says.

"What's that?" Loata asks.

"That's this newly diagnosed mental disorder that give foreigners asthma when they come across locals. That's what wen' happen to the Orange County woman. She had one asthma attack cuz she no could handle being surrounded by all the locals on the green bus."

Dreamhouse

"If I sell sixty more boxes of World's Finest, I can go to Camp Erdman and participate in the Junior Police Officer's annual get-together for free," Vicente says, referring to the chocolate-covered almonds that come in a box with a two-dollar discount coupon from Pizza Hut wrapped around it.

"And you can," Florante says. "I'll help you."

"Me too," Mai-Lan says.

"Me three," Loata says.

After nearly covering the entire valley and hearing the same response of sorry-just-bought-one, Vicente tells Florante, Mai-Lan, and Loata: "I'll try once more before calling it quits."

Knock knock, and a fat lady, wearing glasses so thick they make her eyes look twenty times bigger, answers the door. Vicente pulls out a box of World's Finest and is about to ask her if she wants to buy some when she interrupts, "Too late. Just bought a case the other day. Too late."

He does an about-face to head back home when Mai-Lan comes up with the idea of going to the far end of the valley where people like Stephen Bean live.

"I'm sure we can sell everything in less than a minute," she says.

"Yeah," Florante says, "maybe you might even end up being the top seller and win that AM-FM headset."

It takes them almost an hour's walk to reach the road

that becomes narrower and narrower as the houses get bigger and bigger. The first doors they knock on are all owned by Filipinos like Nelson Ariola's and Prudencio Pierre Yadao's families. They sell over twenty boxes in less than thirty minutes.

Excitedly, they run to the next block where the houses begin to look more like a dream than wooden structures. Like Judy-Ann Katsura's tea house in the middle of a lighted lily pond, and Mr. and Mrs. Bernard Chun's house that Judy-Ann says has an indoor swimming pool with a jacuzzi. After waiting for an eternity, the Katsuras decide to buy seven boxes and the Chuns, three.

Mai-Lan counts the number of boxes sold. "Fifty-seven," she says.

"Three more to go," Florante subtracts.

"And one house left," Vicente adds.

"That's o.k. We still get chance," Loata says, pointing across the field to the biggest house in the valley.

With the heat on their backs, they plod across the field littered with gravel, broken bottles, and thorny weeds. They stop in front of the gate and read the wooden sign drilled through the iron bars. Stenciled in fancy lettering is NO TRESPASSING next to VISITORS, PLEASE RING BUZZER.

Loata rings the buzzer. Mai-Lan and Florante press their faces against the bars that barricade the house. "It's so beautiful and so quiet, like a museum," Mai-Lan says.

"Miniature rolling hills and Hollywood cars," Florante says.

"A fountain with Cupid in the center of a pool," Mai-Lan says.

"A walkway that unfolds like a wedding gown," Florante says.

"It's a dreamhouse."

"Like Iolani Palace with department store windows."

"It looks like Dillingham Prison," Loata blurts. He pushes the button once more and does not let go.

"I don't think anyone's home," Vicente says.

"But get cars park in there," Loata argues, finally releasing his finger from the buzzer.

"Maybe they don't want to buy any chocolate," Vicente says, doing an about-face.

"Look," Loata says, pointing at the giant window where the Beans appear like breathing mannequins on display. Stephen and his mother smile blankly, and his father blows smoke from the cigarette clipped between his fingers. Loata presses the buzzer and waits with his face pushing against the bars.

But not one of the Beans budge. They stand like a Sears family portrait until Stephen's mother walks out of the picture and the drapes begin to close.

BLINDFOLD

He is cruising on the *Love Boat*. He waves to Captain Merrill Stubing and Cruise Director Julie McCoy. They ignore him, walk right through him, straight up to Richard Chamberlain

Pool deck: He is roasting. Richard offers him his Hawaiian Tropic suntan lotion. He turns away

Waves crash into the face of the Pacific Princess, spray his face. Stephen Bean enters his mind. Ocean-blue eyes. He is about to jump into the water. Gopher and Doctor Bricker hold him back

Isaac Washington, the bartender, pours him a glass of Johnny Walker Black Label, straight up with a waterback. Watching Stephen sip a virgin piña colada drink, he orders another Black Label, double-shot, on the rocks

Cocktail lounge: Stephen, dressed in a tuxedo, asks him to slow-dance. Stacy Lattisaw's "Let Me Be Your Angel." He hesitates. Jodie Foster motions to him to accept Stephen's invitation

Stephen takes his hand, leads him to the dance floor. His knees are shaking, palms moist. Stephen holds him by the waist

Don't worry. It's safe here, very safe. Stephen rests his head on his shoulders

The song ends. Tempo changes to an upbeat. "Funkytown." Stephen can't keep up with the beat. He takes Stephen's hands and they touch-dance

Kristy McNichol and Billie Jean King rush to the dance floor. Kristy winks at Stephen, gives him the go-get-'em look. Stephen asks her how she felt kissing Matt Dillon in *Little Darlings*. She turns away

Captain Stubing's daughter Vicki appears. She's crying to Stephen, pulling his arms

How dare you, how dare you, looking past Stephen at him

Stephen tries to explain

Vicki glares at him: Go and snatch someone else's boyfriend, you dirty Filipino homo homewrecker

He pushes Stephen away. Stephen falls. He smashes Vicki's face with a crystal glass

Mr. Roarke and Tattoo welcome him and Edgar to Fantasy Island. Mr. Roarke asks them for their fantasies. He shrugs. Edgar tells Mr. Roarke he's here because Scott Baio wants a second chance. Richard Hatch greets Edgar and the two disappear into the woods

Handing him a vial, Mr. Roarke instructs him to drink the blue elixir before he attends the secret luau. He turns

A door opens onto a dirt road that rolls out like an ancient tongue. An old man, lying on a roll-away bed, hands him a teacup. His voice is hoarse

He takes the cup from the old man's hand and runs his tongue against its porcelain flesh. A man's reflection appears in the cup. He panics, resists, desires, places the cup back on its saucer

The man beckons him to sit beside him: His hand traces the lines around the young man's mouth. The ancient skin awakens his skin, his tongue, his history

A cliff. He panics, wants to jump off, is stopped by a man sitting at the cliff's edge, legs dangling down its face. The man's arms vibrate, the air shakes, shattering the teacup into pieces across the sky

The man's body lifts, propelled out into space by the night

He runs to the edge of the cliff, his arms out. Hands hold him back, rake his hair, massage his chest, the small of his back. Tongues bathe his face, neck, loll in his ears, mouth

Vines sprout between his splayed legs, wrap his body like a shroud, climb his face, masking his mouth and eyes. Praying for air, he bends his head back. In the dark he sees the figure of a man, like a pin of light, moving toward him, blinding him.

SALT

The Men's Public Restroom: Ala Moana Beach Park: Late afternoon. One side of the open-shower area is deserted; the stone benches, unoccupied, dry. On the other side: Transistor radio blares out "Babe" by Styx. Edgar is on his back, tanning to Bain de Soleil. Water streams from a shower head and dives into Vicente's mouth. Standing like a fountain statue, Vicente adjusts the shower knob. Water shoots down to massage his scalp, his neck, his face, to pellet his brows and sting his lips.

A surfer-looking teen clutching a Morey boogie board appears through the veil of water. Tall, muscle-toned, with a rippling stomach, the surfer looks like a local version of Rocky Balboa, with soulful eyes and lips. Vicente turns the shower off.

Edgar cocks an eyebrow as he catches Vicente's eyes trailing after the surfer who, dripping wet, drops his boogie board on the stone bench next to Edgar's. Edgar quickly reaches for the duffel bag beside him and fishes out a pair of sunglasses while his eyes remain fixed at the surfer's back.

Turning down the volume of the radio, Edgar asks the surfer: "Wen' catch any big waves?"

"Nah, small the waves over here," the surfer replies.

"So where you go for surf and boogie board?"

"Normally, I go North Shore."

"You mean like Banzai Pipeline?"

"Yeah, over there and Sunset." The surfer pauses, "Why, you surf?"

"Nah, I just watch the waves," Edgar says, then points to Vicente. "My friend over there bodysurfs. His cousin one professional surfer."

"Who?" the surfer asks.

"Michael Ho."

"For real?"

"For real. Go ask him if you no believe."

The surfer turns his head to Vicente and catches him staring. "Go,"

Edgar nags, "go ask him if you no believe."

As the surfer saunters toward him, Vicente turns around and grabs the shower knob. Water bites into his face. From behind he can feel Edgar's eyes watching him bend his head down as the surfer, smelling of salt, stands next to him.

"Eh, you Michael Ho's cousin?" the surfer asks.

Vicente's heart pounds hard and fast as the surfer asks again, "So you Michael Ho's cousin or what?"

Vicente rubs his eyes with the heel of his palms to blot out the image of the surfer's firm chest, his taut midriff, his pearl-deep navel, and the hairs peeping out of his Lightning Bolt shorts.

"Eh, you deaf or what," the surfer says, then looks over his shoulder at Edgar, who sits up on the bench, watching while he applies suntan lotion on his thighs.

"He no can hear you," Edgar says, crossing his legs to hide his erection. "The water too loud, that's why."

The surfer moves closer to Vicente, who has cupped his hands over his ears and squeezed his eyes shut. "So what, brah, you Michael Ho's cousin or what?"

Vicente's heart pounds harder and faster as the heat of the surfer's breath penetrates the water around him. He bolts out of the shower but slips, his left arm brushing against the surfer's right leg.

"Eh," the surfer shouts out as Vicente disappears behind the wall.

Edgar throws his suntan lotion and beach towel into the duffel bag and sprints after Vicente. "Vicente, dumbass, you forgot your towel," he shouts, then mumbles under his breath, "Shit, that surfer was one fresh and easy catch, too," then, "Vicente, shit, wait for me." But Vicente doesn't hear him. With the imprint of the surfer's skin still smoldering, Vicente races toward the ocean, like lava rushing home.

District
Exemption

"You guys never goin' believe what I just saw and heard," Katrina says as she sits herself between Vicente and Edgar on the bench in front of the 10 Cents Wash & Dry laundromat, located right between the Church of Honolulu and the Pink Store.

"What?" Edgar asks.

"While I was waitin' for my mother for come pick me up after school, I saw Stephen's father walkin' into Principal Okimura's office," she says. "Ho, man, I no could believe. He never even show respect to Okimura-san and he the principal."

The shock in her voice registers front-page news, like a third world war: HIROSHIMA REVISITED: PEARL HARBOR BOMBED AGAIN: GODZILLA VS. KING KONG AT CORREGIDOR.

Edgar and Vicente face her, their hands ready to tug at the string of words she's withholding.

A faint smile crosses her face. Katrina's got their undivided attention. She props her black duffel bag on her lap and slowly unzips it.

"Trina, you irkin' the shit out of me," Edgar snaps. "I know you only tryin' for stall time just so we no need go ice pond."

"No, I not. I just like make sure I never wen' forget my wallet," she says, pretense of worry in her tone.

She fishes out a towel and shakes it. A pink panty

jumps out and trails across the sky for a brief moment before it lands on the pavement in front of the Church of Honolulu. She runs to pick it up.

"Shit," she shouts, holding up the cotton panty smudged with dirt. "Now, I goin' have to wear this inside out."

"Good for you," Edgar says, laughing. "That's what you get for forecastinatin'. Now, sit your ass down and tell us what wen' happen between Principal Okimura and Stephen's father."

She throws the panty with tiny heart-shaped flowers into the duffel bag. "Okay, where was I?" she asks.

"Mr. Bean storming into Principal Okimura's office and throwing tantrums at him," Vicente reminds her.

"Oh, yeah," she says. "Anyways, Bean-head was so pissed off like he was ready for choke Okimura's neck or somethin'."

"Why?" Vicente asks.

"Cuz his cry-baby son wen' tell him what Rowell them guys did to him today at lunchtime," she says, referring to the flattened gecko one of Rowell's bulls had buried in Stephen's pastrami sandwich.

"So that was the straw that finally broke the haole's back," Edgar says. "Stephen so stupid. Nobody told him for get up and go buy one 'nother carton of milk when he already saw Rowell and those guys eyein' his sandwich. How many times already they did that kind stuff to him?"

"I know yeah," she says. "But, ho, man, I wen' peep through the jalousies and I could see the haole was burnin' red. And the kind stuff he was sayin' I no could believe. He was threatenin' for sue everybody, from Rowell them guys to Okimura, and even the Department of Education, unless Okimura give Stephen one district exception for go Kapalama."

"Why, he think the students over there goin' treat him better? Just cuz the school look nice no mean shit," Edgar says.

"And what did Principal Okimura do?" Vicente asks.

"Nothin'. He just wen' stand there and take all that shit Stephen's father was tellin' him," she says.

"Figures," Edgar says. "He's such a wimp. Remember the time Rudy wen' go berserk in class, and Okimura-san no could control him so he ended up calling Officer Hunt? He's such a wimp."

"Oh, and get this," Katrina says. "Stephen's father was so pissed that he was even sayin' stuff about us guys."

"Like?" Vicente asks.

"Like callin' us no-class people," she pauses, "and savages, that was the other word he kept usin'."

"Why, who he think him?" Edgar says.

"One haole," Katrina says.

"One stupid haole," Edgar corrects her.

"Edgar, why do you hate Stephen so much?" Vicente asks.

"Why, you like sleep with him?" he snaps.

"No, I'm serious."

"I serious, too."

"No, really, Edgar, why do you hate haoles so much?"

"I no hate all haoles. Just the kind haoles who think they better than anybody else. You know, the kind who think they still livin' in the time of *Roots*."

"Like the Beans," Katrina interrupts.

"Especially the Beans," Edgar says. "Besides, the word is not 'hate,' Vicente, it's 'pity.' I feel sorry for people like that."

"Well, what about those Filipinos who say they aren't Filipinos?" Vicente asks.

"They in denial," Edgar says.

"What about those Filipinos who act like they're god's gift to other Pinoys?"

"They get one big problem and should go see psychiatrist," Katrina says.

"How come you changed the subject all of a sudden?" Edgar asks.

"What do you mean?" Vicente asks.

"We wasn't talkin' about Filipinos. We was talkin' about haoles—the Beans."

"Aren't they the same; I mean those Filipinos who act like haoles?"

"Vicente?" Edgar says.

"What?"

"Whose side you on?"

"Yeah, Vicente, whose side you on?" Katrina echoes.

"I'm not on anybody's side," Vicente says.

"Maybe you one unconscious two-face or one schizophrenic," Katrina says.

"Shut up, I'm not schizo," Vicente says.

"You shut up," Katrina says.

"How come you get all defensive everytime we razz Stephen down?" Edgar asks.

"I'm not defending anybody."

"Then how come you wen' move the conversation from the haoles to the Flips?"

"I didn't move anything."

"Yes, you did."

"No, I didn't."

"Sometimes I no can figure you out," Edgar says.

"What do you mean, 'figure me out'?" Vicente asks.

"Like you not tellin' us anythin'," Edgar says. "Like we always gotta read between your words."

"You don't gotta read anything," Vicente says.

"Shit, I gettin' tired talkin' to you about this kind stuff," Edgar says. "You ask so many questions; I try for answer 'em as best I can. But you still no catch the drift, or you no like catch the drift. We just better drag our ass to the ice pond right now before my ass get plastered on this bench forever."

The Sentencing Of Lives, Or Why Edgar Almost Failed Mrs. Takemoto's Class

Please form a sentence with the following words. Watch your punctuation. NO PIDGIN-ENGLISH ALLOWED. You have 45 min.

1. nostalgia, n. I get all nostalgia when I listen to Yvonne Elliman's "If I Can't Have You," Andy Gibb's "(Our Love) Don't Throw It All Away," and Auntie Dionne's "I'll Never Love This Way Again."

2. elegy, n. "Tragedy," an elegy included in the Bee Gees' album *Spirits Having Flown,* hit the number-one spot in both *Billboard*'s Pop Singles and Adult Contemporary charts.

3. misinterpret, v. Katrina and I started buying *Song Hits* magazine because we misinterpret a lot of Bee Gees' songs.

4. sobriety, n. When my father drinks and beats the shit out of me, I wish he would be sobriety.

5. vituperative, adj. Our teacher will never be nice because she has a lot of vituperative living in her stomach.

6. sanity, n. I vote my mother as Ms. Hygienic because she always uses her sanity pads when she gets her rags.

7. alienation, n. After defecting the Philippines of Mr. Marcos, Florante's family continues to write in this alienation.

8. quell, v. Nelson Ariola, who comes from a Brady PI Bunch family, is so full of shit that I wish someone would steal his Lightning Bolt ripper wallet, or even better, quell his boto.

9. garrulous, adj. Father Pacheco, alcoholic priest of the century, is very garrulous except when he's listening to our confessions.

10. epiphany, n. Rudy Rodrigues reaches epiphany at least five times a day and he has the needle-tracks record on his arms to prove it.

11. clandestine, adj. In this class is a clandestine boy who freaked out after I gave him a torrid kiss.

12. transition, n. Exotica is in a state of transition at this moment because he wants to undergo a sex change operation so he can enter the Ms. Fusion-Pacifica pageant, but if he does, Daniel, his Air Force loverboy, will leave him.

13. maudlin, adj. My maudlin career is taking off so fast that if I don't try and control it, I'm going to have a nervous breakdown.

14. eliminate, v. After the interview portion, Ms. India had all chances eliminate to become Ms. Universe because she said that if there is one thing she can do to help her country, it is to build a stadium.

15. destitute, adj. Three destitute men were arrested for soliciting the governor's daughter and her cousins on Hotel Street last night.

16. rehabilitate, v. Our teacher wishes she can rehabilitate her mailman-of-a-husband, who is fooling around with Katrina's mother, but she can never will because Trina says only her mother quenches his thirst because that's what he tells her mother before and after they oof.

17. heatwave, n. Exotica's and Daniel's love theme songs are "Dim All The Lights" by Donna Summer and "Always & Forever" by Heatwave.

18. calamity, n. When I think of the hapa-haole fox I make Trina and Loata spy on in the arcade in Mitsukoshi building, my hands get all calamity inside.

19. testimony, n. My testimony is to someday windowshop at Ala Moana Center with his hand in mine.

20. destiny, n. I know this word so close to my heart that it hurts.

Face

Dear Casey Kasem,

You know, I one virgin when come for findin' the right words for explain that what I do and how I feel are not the same. That's why I always listen to the theme song from *Ice Castles*, or buy those expensive cards cuz got rainbows, poems, and all, like the one that says, "Your love brings / endless joy to / my life / I am bound to you," followed by three dots. For infinity. That's why I spend my Sundays countin' down the Top 40 with you when all I waitin' for is really the part where you read the letters that match the song dedications, like the one to the unrequited lover in Missouri, or the runaway father in Cincinnati, or the special, super-duper guy in Nebraska. Frustratin', you know. How many times I tried to write like Susie Polish Shutz, her words so true to my heart? How many times I sent you letters already? I so hungry for this boy, Casey. And even if I one boy when you get to my name, how come, Casey, how come you no pick my letter for the week? I so hungry for this boy. He look like one hapa-Andy Gibb. I see him on the weekends, playin' Galaxian and air hockey at Mitsukoshi game room. He even in my dreams, takin' Scott Baio's place. Such a doll, Casey. Not like the ete guys he hang around with, real bathroom truant types. I tell my friends for scream my name out loud plenty times so he can notice me. But he just walk on by. Slap in the face, Casey. I hate feelin' like this. I hope he stay listenin' so he know the torture I experiencin'. Could you please play "(Our Love) Don't Throw It All Away" by Andy Gibb?

Sincerely yours,
Invisible Edgar

THE SECRET

Edgar thinks it's a secret. He thinks it's a secret because Mr.Campos, the custodian, always tells him that no one else can find out. He thinks no one else can find out because by the time he walks into the janitor's room, everyone has already left the school. Everyone except him and Mr. Campos, who sits on the bench next to the mop stand, waiting with his shirt off and his zipper undone.

Edgar thinks it's a secret because each time Mr. Campos signals him to take off his shirt from Kress or his Toughskins pants from Sears or his rubber shoes from Thom McAn, only he answers to his silent calls. He thinks it's a secret because only he and Mr. Campos know they have just half an hour before the shirt, pants, and shoes must be put on again. He thinks it's a secret because he never sees Mr. Campos' son, who comes to pick Mr. Campos up every day.

Edgar thinks it's a secret when Mr. Campos tells him to lie flat on his stomach or on his back, because only he feels the words. He thinks it's a secret no one can ever find out because it is only his lips and no one else's that Mr. Campos wets, or it is only his neck and no one else's that Mr. Campos licks then blows, or it is only his chest and no one else's that Mr. Campos kisses.

Edgar thinks it's a secret because only he can feel the greying hair brushing against his skin. His skin and no one else's.

Edgar thinks it's a secret Mr. Campos must keep for the rest of his life because Mr. Campos can never tell his wife how Edgar lies flat on his stomach or on his back and runs his tongue on Mr. Campos' cracked lips or licks then blows his neck or kisses his hairless chest.

Edgar thinks it's a secret Mr. Campos can never tell his wife because only Mr. Campos can feel the child's hair, fine as silk, brushing against him. Only he can feel the rejuvenation because only Edgar can feel the white hairs pricking his face.

Edgar thinks it's a secret when Mr. Campos buries his face between Edgar's legs because only Mr. Campos can feel his own heart beating louder and louder as Edgar raises his feet higher and higher. Edgar thinks it's a secret because only he can feel his feet stiffening, his small toes curling. Edgar thinks it's a secret Mr. Campos can never tell because it is forever buried in his mouth, alive and young.

Edgar thinks it's a secret when Mr. Campos, not being able to hold it in, shoots all over him and groans loud enough for the walls to hear.

Edgar thinks it's a secret despite the loud groans. He thinks it's a secret because, though the walls hear him, the walls don't have mouths. He thinks it's a secret because the sound does not escape the room, but echoes again and again in their sighing kisses.

Edgar thinks it's a secret because, though he has to wipe himself with his own shirt, he can always soak it with soap and Clorox as soon as he gets home. He thinks it's a secret because no matter how many times he tries to scrub his body, the smell of Mr. Campos is forever buried in his skin.

Mr. Campos thinks it's still a secret between him and Edgar when Edgar tells Vicente about it. He thinks it's a secret because, before Edgar walks into the janitor's room, he does not hear Edgar telling Vicente to wait until the green door is shut. It's a secret Mr. Campos can never find out because he does not see Vicente watching him through the keyhole. Watching Mr. Campos as he waits on the bench next to the mop stand with his shirt off and his zipper down.

Mr. Campos thinks it's a secret between him and Edgar because he does not see Vicente's eyes each time he signals Edgar to take off his clothes. He thinks only Edgar answers to his silent calls. He thinks only he and Edgar know about the thirty-minute rendezvous.

Mr. Campos thinks it's a secret because he does not know Vicente can see him when he tells Edgar to lie flat on his stomach or on his back. He does not see Vicente's eyes opening wide when he buries his face between Edgar's legs. Vicente's eyes getting wider and wider as Edgar's legs rise higher and higher until toes curl in the air.

Mr. Campos thinks it's a secret when, not being able to hold it in, he shoots all over Edgar and groans. He thinks it's a secret despite the loud groans because, though the walls hear him, the walls don't have mouths. He does not know that, though the walls don't have mouths, the door has eyes.

Mr. Campos thinks it's a secret because he does not see Vicente watching Edgar wipe himself with his own shirt that he soaks with soap and Clorox as soon as he gets home. Mr. Campos thinks it's a secret because he does not see Edgar reaching his arms out and telling Vicente to smell the secret that Mr. Campos thinks is forever buried in his skin.

The Casting

Loata: I tired be Charlie. I no do nothin', that's why. All I do is talk on one speakerphone. No more even haole chicks in bikinis for massage me, not like the real Charlie.

Katrina: You tellin' me. I been playin' Bosley for ages. Eh, Edgar, I like know how come everytime we do *Charlie's Angels* I always gotta be the one for play Bosley? Why no let me be one of the Angels for a change?

Florante: Do you want to be Sabrina because I don't mind playing Bosley.

Katrina: Shit, I take Sabrina Duncan over Bosley anyday.

Edgar: Nonononono. Capital N. O.

Katrina: How come?

Edgar: Cuz you not smart like Sabrina Duncan.

Katrina: What you mean I not smart? I stay in the Hui Akamai Program plus I wen' beat all you guys in the MS Read-A-Thon plus I tops the Spelling Bee contest plus I almost got the Kalihi-Palama Library Reader-of-the-Year Award.

Edgar: What I mean is, you smart but not smart-smart cuz you not multi-lingual like Sabrina Duncan is, like Florante is. Besides, Florante resemble Sabrina Duncan more than you.

Katrina: Yeah, but she one girl and Florante ain't.

Edgar: Yeah, but she look butch enough for pass for one guy.

Katrina: So what you sayin', that I cannot be Sabrina Duncan cuz I no look like one lezbo?

Edgar: Yes.

Katrina: Cuz I more fem than Sabrina?

Edgar: Uh-huh.

Katrina: But not fem enough to be one 'nother Angel?

Edgar: Got it.

Katrina: Which leaves me as Bosley?

Edgar: Bingo.

Katrina: So, in other words, you tellin' me that cuz Sabrina look like one lez I cannot be her cuz I more fem than her but not fem enough for be Kris Munroe or Kelly Garrett. You sayin' that's why every time we play *Charlie's Angels*, I end up playin' Bosley....

Edgar: You gettin' on my nerves, Trina.

Katrina: No make sense to me.

Edgar: Does to me.

Katrina: Doesn't, Edgar, cuz look: I cannot be Sabrina cuz she one lez, and I cannot be Kris or Kelly either cuz they way too fem, but if I be Bosley, that means that Bosley stay somewhere between butch and fem.

Edgar: So?

Katrina: So, in other words, I goin' have to end up playin' Bosley like one fag, and Bosley is far from one fag. 'Sides I no can picture Bosley doin' it with one 'nother guy.

Edgar: Then, what do you picture him as, Ms. Anal-i-tical?

Katrina: Fat and borin' which is not me. Bosley no have sex; I do.

Edgar: Well, use your imagination, that's why God made you the smartest monkey.

Vicente: We're not monkeys; we're apes.

Edgar: MYOB, Vicente, before I make you be Bosley.

Vicente: No, Trina's right. She doesn't match the role of Bosley. Besides, Sabrina Duncan is no longer an Angel.

Katrina: That's right, no? Cuz Kate Jackson left the show so she can pursue her movie career like her husband Andrew Stevens.

Vicente: And she even said so in *The Barbara Walters Special*.

Katrina: (To Edgar) So, see, Florante cannot be Sabrina cuz she no longer part of the show.

Loata: (To Edgar) Jeez, for someone who's always with it, you're a series behind.

Edgar: Oh, shut it. Okay, who you like be then?

Katrina: Well, there's Kris Mun…

Edgar: Up yours. Get only one Kris Munroe here and that's me.

Katrina: Take it easy. No need get all excited; I was only jokin'.

Edgar: Okay, you be Kelly then.

Vicente: Then who am I playing?

Edgar: You be Tiffany.

Vicente: No way, not a chance. I can't stand Tiffany Welles. She's so dense. Talking to her is like talking to air. Why don't you be Tiffany?

Edgar: Why no go fuck a duck?

Vicente: Too late, you beat me to it.

Edgar: Why no go kiss a monkey's ass?

Vicente: Why don't you bend over?

Edgar: See, I knew you was into that. (Vicente pushes Edgar and the two start a push-and-shove match)

Florante: (Pulls Vicente away) Cut it out.

Vicente: I'm sick and tired of him getting his way all the time.

Edgar: You just jealous cuz I get what I want and you never.

Vicente: He can't play boss all the time, and we're letting him call the shots.

Edgar: Like when?

Vicente: Like when we did *Grease*. You had to play Sandy and only Sandy, although Trina, who also wanted to be Sandy, fit the part more because she's the only one who could sing "Hopelessly Devoted To You" like Olivia Newton-John.

Katrina: He right, you know. You always like be the center of attention. Remember when we did *Saturday Night Fever*, you never like none of us be John Travolta?

Edgar: FYI, I was the only one who knew the dance steps to "Night Fever" and "More Than A Woman." Without me, you guys goin' still be dancin' like haoles. Besides, I taught each of you the moves so no tell me I always like be the center of attention. (To Vicente) And you, you of all my bestest bestest friends to talk, you, you two-face closet-case, the many times we did play *Grease*, I can count with my five fingers how many times I was Sandy. (Begins counting) Eight. The rest of the time I wen' let you and Trina be Sandy while I sacrificed to take the second billing as Rizzo.

Vicente: Because you look just like Stockard Channing, I mean, Carol Channing.

Edgar: Oh, excuse me, Mr. *GQ*'s FOB-of-the-Month. FYI, Trina wasn't the only one who wanted for be Sandy. Was you too, you closet-case. You even said so yourself. (Mimics Vicente and gets carried away) "Oh, can be Sandy, please? I know 'Summer Nights' by heart, and I memorize all her lines from my Fotonovel, and I can say 'What's hangin', stud?' to Danny Zuku and mean it, too, and I know all the words to 'You're The One That I Want' and 'We Go Together.' Can play Sandy, please, pretty please?"

Vicente: (Tries to remain calm) Edgar, are you possessed because I swear to God, you're beginning to turn into a Linda Blair from *The Exorcist*. No, make that Linda Blair from *Roller Boogie* since you are getting F-A-T. (Katrina and Loata burst into uncontrollable fits of laughter)

Loata: Oh, that hurts.

Edgar: So what if I gettin' fat? I know I not the same as before. (Katrina and Loata continue laughing) You watch, after two more weeks of *The Richard Simmons Show*, I goin' make you eat your words, Miss In-Denial. (To Loata) Shut it, Sole, it's not like you're God's gift to women, either. Look your bushy hair. Shit, freakin' thing is so bushy, the entire crew of *National Geographic* can live in there. And Trina, you better shut up before I take back all my K-Tel albums I wen' lend you.

Vicente: Keep making threats and you'll run out of friends before you know it.

Edgar: Oh, I'm so afraid. (Sarcastically) The thought of losin' your friendship is so unbearable.

Vicente: Better start bearing it.

Edgar: Oh, you don't know how grateful I am to still have you as my friends. Thank you, thank you so much. I don't know what I ever goin' do without each and every one of you, especially you, Vicente. I never had such a supportive friend who's in the closet before. I want to thank my Mom, Dad, Loata, Florante, Trina, and most of all, my very dear friend, Miss Vicente In-Denial.

Vicente: Don't call me "Miss." I am not a Miss.

Edgar: Okay, Missus then.

Vicente: Fuck you.

Edgar: Fuck you, too.

Loata: Oh shit, here we go again.

Edgar: The nerve of you for cut me down. Mirror, mirror, on the wall, who's the fairiest of us two?

Vicente: ...

Edgar: What, cat got your tongue? At least I know myself better than you do yours. At least I no have to go on pretendin' somethin' that I not.

Vicente: Pretending? I'm not the one who goes around spreading lies.

Edgar: Like what?

Vicente: Like Scott Baio writing you a letter.

Edgar: He did, too. I wrote to his fan club mail and he wrote me back.

Vicente: No, he didn't.

Edgar: Yes, he did. (To Florante, Loata, and Katrina) I even showed you guys, yeah?

Vicente: Yeah, but you didn't tell them you forged the letter that he supposedly sent you.

Katrina: For real, Edgar?

Loata: No joke, Vicente?

Vicente: Yes, he copied Scott Baio's penmanship from *Tiger Beat* magazine.

Loata: Nah.

Katrina: (aside) See, I knew Scott wouldn't take the time of day for sit down and write love letters to one boy.

Edgar: Big Mouth. I knew you can never keep a secret.

Vicente: What secret? That wasn't a secret, Edgar. That was one-hundred-percent pure lie.

Loata: How come you wen' lie to us?

Katrina: Yeah, Edgar.

Edgar: I never lie, I just stretch the truth.

Katrina: Same smell.

Edgar: No, it's not.

Vicente: Yes, it is. You are a liar.

Edgar: Look in the mirror, asshole. What about you? Pretendin' for be straight when you just one 'nother fag like me.

Vicente: I'm not like you. I don't go around bragging to everyone about sleeping with men old enough to be my great-great-grandfather's grandfather.

Edgar: What you talkin' about, "sleeping with old men"? Your wet dreams, Vicente. Maybe you the one like sleep with old men. Not me, I know who to give my youth to.

Vicente: You are such a liar. What about Mr. Campos?

Katrina: Nah, Edgar, you and Mr. Campos wen' oof?

Edgar: No, we never. I would never give my youth up that fast. I not that stupid. 'Sides, he stay married already. Vicente just jealous cuz I can get what I want and he no can.

Vicente: Yeah, the ones who are fifty years older than you.

Edgar: Oh, shut up, you major closet case. You was the very one who wanted for stay longer in the shower cuz you got all hard-up when you saw those naked old men.

Katrina: What shower?

Loata: What naked old men?

Florante: (To Edgar) Stop it.

Edgar: Why no ask the faggot himself?

Loata: What shower?

Vicente: ...

Edgar: The one at Ala Moana Beach Park.

Florante: Stop it, Edgar.

Edgar: No, I not goin' stop now. (To Vicente) I watch you in class. I catch you stealin' glances at the guys' crotch.

Katrina: For real?

Vicente: No, that's not true.

Edgar: That's not true, my ass. I see you lookin' at Stephen Bean in class, liar. I watch the way you pretend for drop your pencil when all you really after is one quick glance at his dick.

Katrina: For real?

Vicente: Don't believe him; he's lying again.

Florante: Let's go. (Grabs Vicente by the elbow and tries to lead him from the group)

Edgar: (Teasingly) Oh, you guys make a cute couple, like Handsome and the Beast. (Vicente turns around and takes a swing at Edgar. Edgar tries to duck but the fist hits him hard on the nose. Startled, Vicente steps back as traces of blood run down his knuckles.)

Katrina: Edgar, your nose stay bleedin'.

Edgar: What? (Wipes his nose with his shirt and sees the bloodstains. Hysterically:) Come on, fucka, you like beef? (Rushes Vicente, who is petrified. Florante shoves Edgar hard.) What, faggot, cannot fight your own battles?

Loata: Stop it, already, Edgar.

Katrina: Yeah, cut it out. Just throw your head back and pinch your nose so the bleedin' goin' stop.

Edgar: (Tips his head back and pinches his nose) Fuckin' fag, he goin' get it. (Vicente and Florante walk away) No matter how many times you like run away from yourself, you cannot.

Loata: (To Vicente and Florante) Hey, you guys, wait up. (The two continue walking)

Edgar: No, Loata, stay. Still early, we can still play *Charlie's Angels*, and this time, you can be Bosley.

Loata: Nah, *Charlie's Angels* can wait til tomorrow. (Runs after Vicente and Florante) Eh, you guys, wait. I comin'.

Katrina: Shit, I goin' too, then. No can have the Angels without Bosley and Charlie.

Edgar: No, stay, Trina. We can play Donny and Marie.

Katrina: For what, Edgar? So you can make me be Donny again?

Edgar: *Facts of Life* then.

Katrina: So you can be Tootie and I can be Natalie?

Edgar: *Laverne & Shirley* then.

Katrina: So you can be Laverne and Shirley, while I play Lenny and Squiggy?

Edgar: Shit, forget it then, you ingrate.

Katrina: Laters. (Runs after Florante, Vicente, and Loata)

Edgar: Go, you backstabber. Go with them. See if I ever make you be Kelly Garrett. (Shouts as they disappear from his sight) You guys just wait, assholes, especially you, you fuckin' faggot. You just wait.

Mama's Boy

Edgar, you knew he was staring. You knew what those hypothyroid eyes meant. But you twitched your ass and made him feel like he was a rainbow, and not Mr. Potato Head with whiteheads the size of Rice Krispies. You twitched your ass, Edgar, because he pretended like it was nothing, like he was not interested, like all he cared about was watering his medium-sized belly with a six-pack of Primo beer.

Don't try to deny it, Edgar, because I saw you watch him bend over to wax his yellow car. And I saw you get mad when he took his fat fingers off the rag and looked away. You got mad, Edgar, so you started pulling the ends of your shorts high and wouldn't stop until you caught him grinning. I told you, Edgar, what are you doing? Stop it, Edgar. He's staring. But did you stop? No, you didn't. You went on, dancing and twirling and throwing your head back.

You pulled your shorts higher the minute the Mr. Softee truck turned onto our street. You pulled them so high they looked like a bikini. You even showed him your tan-line, Edgar. And when he flashed you a five-dollar bill and pointed to the toolshed, you acted like he was suddenly the most important person in your life. No, Edgar, I said. But you said, Goin' only take few minutes, Vicente. Whistle if you see his mother.

I should've gone home, Edgar. I shouldn't have stayed. I only stayed because I was scared for you. But when you two came out after a minute, you made like it was nothing, like you went in to watch cartoons and got bored. I asked you, Did he hurt you? And all you said was, He never do nothin'; his eyes never even fall off. Then you laughed because he told you, Your friend, I like your friend. You're not funny, I said. But you said, Go, Vicente, he goin' give us twenty bucks, that's why.

I was leaving when you grabbed my arm. Let go, I said. Look, you said, he showin' us twenty bucks. Stop it, he's staring, I said. No, Edgar, he wasn't staring at me. It was you he was looking at with those pinball eyes. It was you he really wanted. But you said, Twenty bucks, Vicente, we can go Castle Park with that.

That's a lie, Edgar. You wouldn't let go of my arm. You even begged me. You said, Please, Vicente, he not goin' do nothin'. I don't want to, I said. I'm scared. No be, you said. He one mama's boy, and mama's boy only like touch. Hurry before he change his mind. You made it sound so easy, like TV dinners ready in three minutes. You said, No worry, Vicente, I goin' be right by the door. I promise. I not goin' move. You better, I said.

I thought I was going to die in there, Edgar. So dark, so stuffy. He was sweating. I stayed because I was afraid he was going to hurt you. I was scared, Edgar, but he said, You scared of me? No need be scared of me. I not goin' hurt you. I only like touch Filipino birdie.

He rubbed my head, Edgar, my face. I was so scared, Edgar. He touched my chest, so slow. His hands were waxy, Edgar. I smelled them. Like his yellow car. Edgar, Edgar, I yelled. Shhh, he said. He grabbed my wrist. The money is in here. I couldn't breathe. So dark. Let go, I said. Not until you find it. My hand, Edgar. What you waitin' for? Pull it.

Where were you, Edgar? Why did you leave me? It should've been you in there. Yes, Edgar, you. You were the one who teased him. You were the one who wanted that hot fudge sundae, that twenty dollars for Castle Park. It should've been you, Edgar, not me. You wanted it. You deserved it. Not me, Edgar. Not me.

Heart

How dare you guys give me the same freakin' gifts this Christmas? Think I no shop at Longs? Think I no check how much those damn storybook containin' five rolls of Lifesavers candies cost? Ninety-nine cents plus four-percent tax, assholes. Til this day, I still in shock.

What the fuck I goin' do with twenty-five rolls of Lifesavers? I wasn't expectin' the Three Kings for come kneel in front my manger. I not picky. But twenty-five freakin' rolls Lifesavers? Even my mother freaked out, said, "Edgar-anak, you goin' be suckin' those candies til your teeth fall off. Better go give 'em to Father Pacheco cuz he still collectin' donations for give to the poor. 'Sides, your father just wen' pau payin' off the dentist." So I did. I gave 'em all to the poor with all my heart.

No give me that stink look, like I never appreciated your gifts. Shit, how would you feel if I gave each of you five rolls of SweeTarts for Christmas? You guys so full of shit. What you mean it's the thought that counts? Try like it's your tightass wallet that counts. You guys sure you not Chinese? No tell me so long thing comin' from the heart.

I almost went around the island thinkin' what for give you guys, gifts I know goin' make you happy cuz I never missed one single clue thrown at me like: "Oh, I love David Naughton, he way better than Rupert Holmes or Andy Gibb, I love the song 'Makin' It.' I wish I had the 45's."

Trina, I went through hell and back just for make your damn wish come true. I had to bus 'em all the way to Pearlridge cuz the DJ's at Ala Moana and Dillingham never had the 45's. Plus the freakin' bus wasn't air-conditioned.

For you, Mai-Lan, I know I only got you one five-dollar book certificate from McDonald's that came with the free calendar, but be grateful the truck driver saw me jaywalkin' just in time, or else you never goin' get that free small fries if you buy a Big Mac come July.

For you, Vicente, for get you that cellophaned magazine only sold in the bookstore down Hotel Street, I had to get one fake ID first, cuz the owner fired my friend Dirty Harry Kajimoto after he got caught sellin' mags to juveniles. I know never had to be *Strapped Jocks,* but I wanted to cuz this the mag that wen' help me come out of the closet, and I confident goin' help you out, too. Shit, I should've kept that mag for myself if only I knew all you was goin' give me was five rolls Lifesavers.

For you, Loata, I got bad lickens from my father cuz I wen' close my Honolulu Federal Savings Eagles Club account just so I can buy that Mongoose bike you been wantin' since god-knows-when. I know you the Talofa sheep in the family, but why you never just tell your mother for bake me one banana bread instead of givin' me those freakin' candies. Oh, I so piss off.

And as for you, Florante, poet of my heart, I know you not the type for accept expensive gifts, but I was garanz the *Grease* soundtrack cassette goin' help you a-cult-too-late the American culture. I no mind you givin' me one storybook Lifesavers candies cuz, after all, it did come in five different flavors, includin' spearmint for when I tongue-kiss. But why you had to jump into their bumper cars for? Why never just dedicate me one of your poems even if I no understand?

There, it's all out. Shit, I still piss off. You guys better shut up and no give me that crap about better to give than receive cuz now I know for a fact you guys only take take take and never ever give give give. Wait til next Christmas.

CHAIN LETTER TRANSLATED FROM SAINT MALAS

THIS LETTER HAS BEEN SENT TO YOU FOR GOOD LUCK BECAUSE WE LOVE YOU. WE REALLY DO. AND WE WANT YOU TO LIVE A FRUITFUL, PAIN-FREE, AND BLISSFUL LIFE. THIS IS WHY WE ARE SENDING YOU THIS LETTER. THE ORIGINAL IS NOW IN HORSESHOE BEND, IDAHO. A COPY OF THIS LETTER HAS GONE AROUND THE WORLD NINETY-NINE TIMES.

TREMENDOUS LUCK IS ON YOUR WAY WITHIN FOUR DAYS UPON RECEIVING THIS LETTER, PROVIDED THAT YOU PASS IT ON TO OTHERS WHO YOU THINK NEED GOOD LUCK. THIS IS NO LAUGHING MATTER. DO NOT SEND MONEY, FOR FAITH HAS NO PRICE. DO NOT KEEP THIS LETTER. IT MUST LEAVE YOUR HANDS WITHIN NINETY-SIX HOURS.

DUSTIN HOFFMAN RESPONDED TO THE CHAIN TWO DAYS BEFORE THE OSCAR CEREMONY AND WON THE BEST ACTOR AWARD FOR *KRAMER VS. KRAMER;* ROY SCHNEIDER, ON THE OTHER HAND, LOST FOR *ALL THAT JAZZ* BECAUSE HE BROKE THE CHAIN.

MS. USA OBEYED THE CHAIN AND WAS REWARDED THE COVETED TITLE OF MS. UNIVERSE. IN THE PHILIPPINES, THE WIFE OF LT. NORMAN CHANDLER OF CLARK AIR FORCE BASE WAS MUTILATED INTO A THOUSAND PIECES JUST TEN DAYS AFTER HER HUSBAND RECEIVED THIS LETTER BECAUSE HE IGNORED IT. HOWEVER, BEFORE HER

DEATH, HE RECEIVED $8,944,703.05 THEN LOST IT.

PLEASE SEND TWENTY COPIES AND SEE WHAT HAPPENS. THE CHAIN ORIGINATED FROM CEBU AND WAS WRITTEN IN 1521 BY SAINT RICARDO MALAS, A COLONIZER-TURNED-MARTYR FROM SPAIN. SINCE THIS COPY MUST TOUR THE WORLD, YOU MUST MAKE TWENTY COPIES AND SEND THEM TO YOUR FRIENDS, FAMILIES, AND FOES. AFTER A FEW DAYS, YOU WILL GET A BIG SURPRISE. THIS IS TRUE EVEN IF YOU ARE NOT SUPERSTITIOUS, CATHOLIC, OR FILIPINO.

DO NOTE THE FOLLOWING: FERDINAND MARCOS RECEIVED THE CHAIN ON THE EVE OF THE 1968 PRESIDENTIAL ELECTION. HE ORDERED HIS MAIDS AND COHORTS TO PRODUCE 1,220 HANDWRIT-TEN COPIES. HE WON THE ELECTION BY A LANDSLIDE, AND TIL THIS DAY, HE STILL RULES THE COUNTRY VIA MARTIAL LAW.

WITH LOVE AND QUICK RESPONSE, LUCK WILL ALWAYS BE ON YOUR SIDE. REMEMBER: DO NOT IGNORE THIS. IT WORKS.

ST. JUDE

P.S. Florante, if you like win the poetry contest...
P.P.S. Katrina, you ready for be one sixth grade mother...
P.M.S. Mai-Lan, kiss the red room goodbye if...
M.S.G. Stephen, world will start loving you if...
S.O.S. Vicente, remember the man in the yellow car...
M.I.C. Loata, you might never see your bike again...
F.O.B. Nelson, you can be one full-on American if...
F.Y.I. Maggie, if you like hang on to Christopher...

F FOR BOOK REPORT

Some important things to keep in mind when doing a book report are: What is the plot? Who is the main character? Does he/she get what he/she wants? Are there any obstacles preventing him/her from attaining his/her goal? Is the conflict internal or external? Man vs. Man? Man vs. Nature? Man vs. Self? Any relation between the story and the title of the book? Is there a moral to the story? Would you recommend the book? Why or why not?

Remember: Your job is to give a brief, yet concise summation of the book. DO NOT RE-TELL THE STORY. Underline the title of the book. AND REMEMBER: NO PIDGIN-ENGLISH ALLOWED.

My book report is on Judy Blume's <u>Forever: A Moving Story of the End of Innocence</u>. The story is about Katherine Danziger and Michael Wagner, two high-school seniors who meet at Sybil's fondue party then fall in love with each other the following morning. Katherine is the main character in the book. So is Michael, but Katherine is more of a main main character than Michael because <u>Forever</u> is more of her story than his. Katherine goes to Westfield High and lives with her parents and her younger sister Jamie, who is very much into the arts. Michael attends Summit High. Sybil is their common friend.

<u>Forever</u> is one of the bestest bestest books I ever read cuz it's so true-to-life and I know it cuz I lived it. I feel like I know Katherine so well, even though I one local and she live all the way east coast side, cuz I can fully relate to the things that happen to her from page one to page two hundred twenty. Was kinda scary actually, reading this book, cuz felt like I was reading about myself. For one thing, we get the same name, except she get haole last name, Danziger, and mine's Cruz, as in Katherine Kat-

rina-Trina Cruz. She in twelfth grade while I stuck here in fifth. Secondly, we both get boyfriends. Hers is Michael Wagner, and mine, of course, is none other than Erwin Castillo, star quarterback for the undefeated Farrington Govs. And last but not least, we both mature—not like the 99.9% students in this dumb, boring class.

At first, Katherine try for pretend she not really into Michael, but after two chapters, she stay letting him hold her hand and touch her boobs and here and there, but not her tight bilat cuz she still one virgin, not like her friend Sybil who's this full-on slut. I feel kinda sorry for Sybil cuz all she do is spread spread spread and she forget who she spreading to. In the end, Sybil get pregnant but gotta give the baby away for adoption cuz she no like get one abortion cuz she say she want for experience childbirth. Sybil, she not too smart. That's why she not the main character.

Erica, Katherine's bestest bestest friend, is also not the main character, but she a little bit more developed than Sybil, just a little bit more, cuz she start off as one virgin and end up as one. That's not her fault though. See, Erica stay checking out this guy Artie, Michael's friend. She get the hots for him. She all ready for spread for him every time they meet. I mean, she want Artie for end her innocence, but Artie, he act just like one fag. I feel for Artie, especially cuz he don't know what and who he is. And his father is one real dick cuz he no like Artie be one actor, even though he played lead in the senior play. That's why he attempt suicide in the end. I feel more for Erica, though, cuz she all ready, but til this day, she still one virgin.

Like I already mentioned before, Forever is a love story between Katherine and Michael. They meet. He like oof her. She say no. They meet again. Again, she pretend she not itchy. Instead, she just make him feel her up. But one night, she so horny, she let him finger her bilat and she let him let her pet Ralph, that's the name Michael gave to his dick.

That part was unbelievable for me. Maybe cuz when my babe Erwin first showed me his boto, he never said stuffs like, Trina, I like you meet Rudolfo, my big boto. I swear only haole guys would name their botos Ralph. Only haole guys would give their botos names period.

That's not the only problem with Michael. Even though I imagine him as one foxy babe like Rex Smith, I would never let Michael pop my cherry. His boto might be super big, but he's boring in bed. For example, when Katherine finally ready for loosen up, Michael go inside her but he stay there for only one minute cuz he wen' already ejaculate. He never even give her chance for scream. He's so boring. Anyways, by then, it's too late for Katherine for turn back cuz she got poked already and stay bleeding. The first time Erwin was inside me, I thought he was never going let me get up and use the bathroom. He's so good, I no can wait for see him.

After Katherine experience what it means to be a woman, she start itching for Michael for oof her everytime they get together. She feel so free and womanized, she start experimenting with Michael's Ralph in the shower, the den, his sister's bedroom. She like oof everytime, yet each time they do it, Michael come too soon. He's so junk. He only good for the first round. Only once he never let her down, and that time, she come twice. She boring, too.

When Erwin and I make love, we foreplay first. I talking about tongue-kissing, ball-tickling, ear-licking, everything. None of this Ralph shit. And we do more than just stand in the shower and pretend we from Greece in the olden days. Erwin not into that kind stuff. He rather do me way up Tantalus in the back seat of his father's Toyota truck, or at the Chinese graveyard in Manoa. I like it when we make out at Ala Moana Beach Park late late at night, almost morning but not quite cuz the senior citizens not out walking and jogging yet. He so strong when he touch me, and I let him be cuz I know what a man needs.

Anyways, Katherine and Michael start getting into the other heavy-duty stuff, which is relationship. These guys only known each other for couple months and already they acting like they no can live apart. I believe them, though, cuz that's how you supposed to feel when you in love, when you open yourself up to someone important cuz you have this strong feeling he never going let you down, or hurt you. But Katherine's parents start freaking out. They so overprotective. They scared Michael going steal their daughter forever, so they make her spend the whole summertime working as one assistant tennis counselor at one summer fun camp in New Hampshire. I never even know Katherine play tennis.

I lucky my mother no try separate me and my babe Erwin. Probably cuz she know Erwin not dicking around when he say he love me in front her. And he no like me get pregnant, too. So every time we go all the way, he always bring his box of rubbers cuz he no like me get pregnant too young too soon. I love him so much. I no can wait for see him. And we call each other babe, too. Other times, he call me hon, and I call him JMV, cuz he look just like Jan-Michael Vincent. Ho, that's one other babe. After I saw Big Wednesday, I pray that someone like him going oof me next. Richard Hatch is one other babe. So is Christopher Reeve.

Anyways, a week or two after Katherine go summer camp with her sister Jamie, she start checking out this guy Theo, the head of the tennis program. At first I thought she just itchy cuz Michael stay all the way in North Carolina, and I know exactly how she feel cuz sometimes I get itchy, too, like when Erwin gotta go Big Island for visit his grandparents. But I soon realize that when two lovers get separated for too long a time, the feelings might change. That's what happens to Katherine. She meet Theo, and she get into deep shit cuz her heart stay throbbing for Theo while her mind stay telling her, wait wait wait for Michael.

I recommend this book especially for you, Mrs. Takemoto, cuz you might learn a thing or two about love and the painful truth that nothing last forever, not even love. I know you know and everybody know that your husband stay screwing my mother. That's how come you hate my guts so much. I can be one bitch, too, like my mother, and tell you that the main reason why your husband rather sleep in our house is that my mother get one hourglass figure and you need to exercise with Richard Simmons then go Merle Norman afterwards.

But that's beside the point. What I trying for say is the same thing that my mother tell me everytime about me and Erwin. She tell me that if Erwin no love me no more, I should tell him to fuck off, that I should move on with my life, cuz I only going be miserable the whole time I stay hanging on to him. I say the same thing to you, Mrs. Takemoto. Why hang around somebody when he like you out of his sight? You only wasting your time.

You might think I making this up only to piss you off, only so my mother can have your husband all to herself, but I not. I know what your husband want and need, and I hate for be the one to tell you this, but it ain't you but my mother. He said so himself plenty times. He said he no can wait for you for file one divorce cuz he so tired of him going home to you cuz you always give him the third degree. And I also hate for be the one to tell you that there's love between my mother and your husband. That's why they no care what everybody saying about them. But, like I said before, love don't last forever. Who knows? Maybe your husband going wake up one morning and find that he no longer get feelings for my mother. Maybe vice-versa.

As for me, my heart stay with Erwin. Our relationship ain't perfect. He graduating this year, I moving up to sixth. Now and then, we get into fights. He threaten me with his fist and I kick his balls. I don't know if he going be the one shouting I do I do I do to me in front Father Pacheco. That's too far ahead to be thinking about. But for now, I just gotta make the most of Erwin, cuz for now, Erwin is my forever.

R. Zamora Linmark lives in Honolulu.